Christmas
at the
Vicarage

REBECCA BOXALL

Christmas
at the
Vicarage

LAKE UNION
PUBLISHING

Text copyright © 2015 Rebecca Boxall

Published by Lake Union Publishing, Seattle

www.apub.com

Amazon, the Amazon logo, and Lake Union Publishing are trademarks of Amazon.com, Inc., or its affiliates.

ISBN-13: 9781503948402
ISBN-10: 1503948404

Cover design by bürosüd° München, www.buerosued.de

Printed in the United States of America

In memory of Dad (Diddle)
And for my girls, Ruby and Iris

PROLOGUE
OCTOBER 2014

'He speaks in dreams, in visions of the night,
when deep sleep falls on people as they lie in their beds.'
Job 33:15 (NLT)

Rosamunde stood calmly at the shoreline. She watched the seals bob up and down in the distance and, for this moment, everything seemed right with the world. So still. So peaceful. Until suddenly it wasn't.

In an instant she realised the figures weren't seals at all – they were people. She knew them at once: there was her father and, next to him, her mother, Marguerite. Circling them like seagulls were Rachel, Kizzie, Stephen, Mrs Garfield and Benedict.

It was a bright summer's day; there hadn't been a single blemish in the sky and yet somehow an enormous black cloud had emerged from nowhere and the swimmers had almost simultaneously begun to panic. Rosamunde started to strip off her clothes; she simply had to help them, but her limbs felt heavy and as she lumbered into the sea she felt weighed down by an almighty force of gravity. As she swam into the deep waters she knew there was one person she must save first – someone who would drown if she didn't get there soon.

Suddenly, Rosamunde was awake, sweating, her heart pounding with adrenalin. It was the same dream she'd had all week and she was never closer to knowing the answer to the critical question: who was the person she needed to save?

PART ONE

PART ONE

1.

SUNDAY 16TH NOVEMBER 2014

She'd been gone for fifteen years and was now in her forties. But the dreams, recurring night after night, had finally drawn her home. They'd been like an invisible lasso, pulling her tighter and harder until Rosamunde had inevitably found herself first at Perth International Airport, then at Heathrow, Paddington, Totnes and, finally, the small station of Thatchley, just ten minutes from Potter's Cove.

Thatchley was so quaint it was the kind of place used by the BBC when it required a suitably old-fashioned station for a period drama. However dishevelled and travel-weary you felt, it was impossible not to feel the antique glamour of the place on arriving. Rosamunde, who by now looked decidedly unglamorous, lugged her various bags onto the platform and breathed slowly and deeply. Dark, crisp November air. With one breath she was filled with memories of bonfire nights past – fingerless gloves, sticky toffee apples, fizzing sparklers and piping hot jacket potatoes. Already her memory had been stirred and she hadn't even reached Potter's Cove.

She heaved her bags along the platform and bypassed the ticket office, taking the side gate towards the main road. As hoped, her shortcut won her the only waiting taxi and, rather gleefully, she opened the boot and had stowed her luggage before the driver – a funny-looking man with an enormous nose and (it turned out) dreadful halitosis – managed to hoist himself from his seat to help her. As she clambered into the back seat she spotted a couple of other train passengers emerging from the ticket office and looking hopefully about them. Rosamunde knew they would have a long wait for another taxi but she refused to feel guilty. After all, no one else could possibly have endured as lengthy a journey as her.

The drive took no time at all and yet seemed never-ending. As the taxi wound through the tiny Devon roads that squiggled down into the village and back up the small hill to the Vicarage, the driver slowed to an agonising snail's pace. Rosamunde found herself willing the man to drive faster. She could hardly bear to wait a moment longer.

'Could you possibly go a little faster?' she called out to the front.

'Sorry, love,' said the man, though he didn't sound very sorry. 'More than my job's worth.'

Rosamunde was not argumentative by nature, but even she had to bite her tongue, quite literally, to prevent herself from replying to this unhelpful response.

And then, suddenly, they were there. With the driver paid and the bags man-handled from the boot, Rosamunde hurried to the back door ('family and tradesmen,' her mother had always said, mocking her own aristocratic heritage). She was here. Her back ached and her eyes were gritty but, finally, she was here.

The thatched cottage glowed in the moonlight. It was unusually picturesque for a vicarage – an ancient cottage that had been spared being sold off by the Church when the more usual Victorian vicarages were considered too expensive to upkeep and had been replaced with modern bungalows. It had thick walls that kept the sea damp at bay and, while cosy, it had everything a grow-ing family could require: an eat-in kitchen with Aga, a larder, a small utility and a downstairs loo; a well-proportioned sitting room with a working fireplace; a small study; and a creaky staircase leading upstairs to four reasonably sized bedrooms, though there was only one bathroom – which had caused a few squabbles over the years. The best thing of all, though, was the position of the cottage – perched above the village, suitably close to the little church, and with a sweeping view of Inner and Outer Cove – the magnificent beach below that divided into two as the tide drew in.

Rosamunde smiled and took a deep breath of sea air. She opened the back door. And there in the kitchen, studying the dishwasher, was the Reverend Bernie Pemberton.

'Rosamunde?' he asked, peering short-sightedly at her. Then, satisfied she wasn't a figment of his imagination, he yelped with delight.

'I wasn't sure what time you'd be home!' Bernie exclaimed as he pulled his daughter into a bear hug. He smelt utterly comforting. Of washing powder and Polo mints and, most of all, just her dad. Stepping back to appraise him, she felt a lump of sadness rise suddenly to her throat as she realised how much older he looked, with his shock of white hair that had once been so red. Like a physical weight it hit her just how much of his life she'd missed over the last fifteen years. The brief visits she'd made in that time hadn't been enough.

'But you're back, dear girl, you're back,' Bernie said, as though reading her mind. 'Now tell me, have you looked at the crossword yet? It's a beast today and I need your help.'

A marvellously decadent hour followed. The pair toasted themselves by the crackling log fire as they sipped scalding tea, with their heads in the *Telegraph* and Gladys the cat at their feet. After a while Rosamunde stretched her arms and surveyed the cosy surroundings of the home she'd escaped from, bursting as it had been with bittersweet memories. After many years away she'd finally begun to wonder if the geography was irrelevant. The memories could never really disappear. The best you could hope for was that they would fade, and lose their power, with time.

The sitting room was exactly as it had always been – a room as bright and sunny in the summer months as it was snug and welcoming in winter. Two squashy gold sofas faced each other on either side of the fireplace and a low coffee table – usually heaving with newspapers and mugs – occupied the space between the two. Directly opposite the fireplace were the French windows, leading to the walled garden at the back of the cottage, which were dressed with pretty crimson curtains.

To the left of the French windows was a corner shelf crammed with books as diverse as the *Holy Bible, Delia's Christmas* and the poetry of Byron, and an array of well-thumbed novels. A low, beautifully upholstered chair was placed beside the bookshelf for the convenience of anyone who might wish to perch and scrutinise the blurbs on the back covers, deciding whether to borrow this novel or that.

In another corner, affixed to two walls, was a dark oak corner cupboard containing ancient glasses – sherry, champagne, port and wine – all gifts Rosamunde's parents had received for their wedding. Beneath the cupboard was a shining chestnut table, lovingly polished over the years, upon which a tray lay invitingly, housing a selection of bottles to suit varying tastes – as long as they were alcoholic.

It was a pleasing room, decided Rosamunde, as she sighed contentedly and sat back against the sofa.

'But I'm a terrible host, even to my own daughter,' Bernie piped up suddenly, dismayed. 'You must be exhausted after your journey. Have a bath – there's plenty of hot water – and come back down when you're ready. There's a bottle of champagne in the fridge with your name on it,' he added, ruffling Rosamunde's long red hair just as he'd always done. 'My dear girl, I'm so glad you're home.'

'Me too, Dad,' Rosamunde replied. 'I really am,' she added with a smile. And, as she said it, she realised just how much she meant it. How on earth had she stayed away so long?

Yawning hugely, Rosamunde climbed the rickety stairs to her childhood bedroom, with Gladys following in hot pursuit. She opened the creaky wooden door and was taken aback to find the room had been refreshed.

The curtains had been an old Laura Ashley pair but in their place were fresh white drapes with a discreet pattern of daisies embroidered along the hem. Her single bed had been replaced with a small double and was covered with starched white linen and a pretty coloured blanket for extra warmth. Opposite the bed, on the pine chest of drawers, was a terracotta jug filled with scarlet and purple anemones.

It was warm and homely and had the definite feel of a woman's touch, but if there was a new woman in her father's life she was certainly sensitive, for beside the bed stood a freshly polished silver frame encasing a black and white photograph of Rosamunde's mother. There she sat, gazing serenely with her enormous black eyes at the photographer, her dark hair cut into a gamine crop. It had been taken just before she died and captured Marguerite at the height of her beauty.

Later on, warmed by a bath in the old-fashioned roll-top and emboldened by the delicious champagne, Rosamunde tentatively probed her father on the subject.

'My bedroom's looking very pretty,' she remarked, taking a large mouthful of piping hot shepherd's pie. They were sitting at the scrubbed kitchen table in the corner of the kitchen, tucked snugly beside the old red Aga.

'Ah yes, as soon as we knew you were coming home we decided to freshen things up a little for you. I'm glad you like it.'

'We?' Rosamunde asked. She held her breath.

'Yes, me and Mrs Garfield, of course. She still helps me in the house. She was here this afternoon, in fact. Left just before you arrived but sends you her love. Such a treasure. Who did you think I meant?'

'Oh, no one,' Rosamunde replied. She felt unaccountably disappointed. Since their mother had died Rosamunde and her sister had often wondered if their father would remarry. Initially the thought had horrified them and they'd made sure to be as unpleasant as possible whenever anyone remotely pretty was invited for tea. But as time went by they had begun to hope he might one day find someone to keep him company once they left home.

Rosamunde had forgotten that, of course, Mrs Garfield was the only womanly touch in the Vicarage. Dear Mrs Garfield, the domestic help for as long as Rosamunde could remember. Indeed, more than just a help. A comfort. A shoulder to cry on. As round and squashy as a doughnut, sweet as the jam in the middle, but fiercely efficient and hard-working.

Rosamunde opened the bathroom door the next morning and was surprised to stumble upon a Mrs Garfield who'd undergone an even more dramatic transformation than her childhood bedroom. Where her plain but cheerful face had previously been framed with a mass of grey, frizzy curls, a glossy chestnut bob was now tucked behind her ears, making her subtly made-up eyes gleam with life. Also long gone were the comforting curves Rosamunde remembered: Mrs Garfield's svelte new figure was wrapped in indigo boot-cut jeans and a crimson jumper.

'You look like you've seen a ghost!' shrieked Mrs Garfield, dropping the can of polish in her hands and gathering Rosamunde into a hug that was no less all-encompassing for her newly slender frame.

'But Mrs G,' gasped Rosamunde, stepping back to assess her old friend again. 'You're like a new woman!'

'Get away with you! I'm still the same underneath,' Mrs Garfield smiled, clearly pleased with the compliment. 'GHDs, you know,' she added in her wonderfully confidential manner. Rosamunde looked lost.

'You know! Hair straighteners! That frizzy mop of mine is a thing of the past. Mr Garfield passed away a couple of years ago now and your sister took me to one side after the funeral and told me it was "now or never", and that if I took a train to London she'd give me a free makeover.'

Rosamunde rolled her eyes and smiled at Rachel's famous tactlessness and sense of timing. A flamboyant whirlwind of vitality, Rachel was a force to be reckoned with.

'Rachel gave me all this information about what colours and styles suit me, how I should do my hair – she even gave me some old GHDs of hers. Then we went shopping for make-up. Next thing I did when I got back to Potter's Cove was sign up for Weight Watchers at the church hall, and here I am, just turned sixty and never felt so good!'

'I'm impressed,' said Rosamunde. 'But listen, why don't we go downstairs and have a cup of tea and you can tell me what else has been going on in the last fifteen years?'

A wonderfully gossip-fuelled breakfast followed with Bernie – who was multi-tasking by half-heartedly preparing a sermon with one eye, while fixing the other on the crossword – contributing to Mrs G's debrief. Once satisfied she'd been brought fully up to date, Rosamunde decided to take a walk straight down to Outer Cove below.

As she strolled along, she marvelled at the changes she'd already encountered, changes she somehow hadn't expected. To her, Potter's Cove and everyone in it had remained as they'd been fifteen years ago when she'd left at the age of twenty-eight, visiting only briefly and infrequently since.

Rosamunde tucked her dark red hair into her velvet coat, so that it acted as a scarf in the absence of a woollen one, and braced herself for her first close-up of the cove. Here, standing at the edge of the slipway and peering down at the waves crashing angrily onto the shore below, she finally gave herself over to her memories. It was like releasing a dam: the floodgates had opened.

2.

JULY 1978

The summer of 1978 was the gloomiest summer Rosamunde and Rachel had ever known. The sun beat down oppressively but their hearts were cold and heavy. They wondered if life would ever be normal again. At the funeral they were as quiet as mice. They were so in awe of the enormous crowds that neither of them shed a tear. Rosamunde was naturally shy and could hardly bear to look at anyone, but if she glanced up for a moment she noticed the pitying, inquisitive looks on every single face. All she could hear were murmured whispers.

'Poor little things. Look at them,' and 'Little Rosamunde, only seven years old,' and 'How will he cope, I wonder?' They all whispered too loudly. Rosamunde wished she could stuff cotton wool in her ears. She started to hum until her dad told her, very gently, to be quiet. He had red, puffy eyes. She didn't like it.

At the burial, at least, the girls were surrounded only by close family. Standing by the side of the great hole in the ground Rosamunde felt hot and uncomfortable. The sun was unforgiving and the vicar kept mopping his brow with a spotty handkerchief. Normally her dad was the vicar but today someone else was. Dad said it was because he was too sad to speak. She didn't think she was going to cry but then Rachel started tickling her. It was a strange thing to do; perhaps her sister was desperate to hear laughter. But instead Rosamunde started crying.

She became inconsolable and, as the coffin was lowered, found herself becoming quite hysterical. This behaviour was so uncharacteristic (it was usually Rachel who was prone to histrionics) that her father and grandmother weren't sure what to do with her. In the end Granny Dupont threatened to smack her bottom unless she was quiet. Rosamunde thought this was very mean in the circumstances but she began to quieten down. Tears still streamed down her face, though, and she noticed Rachel's face was wet and blotchy too. She wondered if they would spend every day crying now instead of laughing and the thought made her tummy ache.

But as the days passed, Rosamunde realised that life carried on. They were all a little quieter and a little sadder, but the sun still shone and Bernie still had to work. September came and the girls were required to return to school. Nothing would ever be quite the same without the loving arms of their mother to comfort them, but they got on with their lives. There didn't seem to be any alternative.

∽

Three years later, in July 1981, the whole country was in a state of mass celebration. It was the day of Prince Charles and Lady Diana's wedding.

'*Please* will you play Sindys with me,' Rosamunde begged her sister. She loved playing Sindys with Rachel. Whilst the families Rosamunde created were unfailingly conventional, Rachel always invented thrilling characters and thought her sister exceedingly boring.

Rosamunde could feel tears of frustration starting to prickle at her eyes and tried to blink them away. Rachel hated tears. In fact Rosamunde hadn't seen Rachel cry since the day of their mother's funeral. Since then Rachel had been so determinedly cheerful Rosamunde sometimes thought she might strain her face through smiling and laughing. Rosamunde felt dreadfully feeble by comparison.

'I've already told you,' Rachel said in her newly acquired, patronising tone, 'I'm way too old for Sindys. Jeepers, Rosamunde, I'm thirteen now! Anyway, this is *the* most important day of the year. I can't believe you're even considering playing Sindys when Prince Charles and Lady Di are getting married today.' Rachel glared at her sister and noticed Rosamunde's watering eyes.

'Oh for goodness' sake!' she exclaimed. 'Rosamunde, if you don't stop crying I'll tell Granny Dupont.' This managed to stop the tears in their tracks as they slithered down Rosamunde's cheeks. Granny Dupont's name made her sound like some sort of cosy French grandmother with rosy cheeks and hair pulled back into a practical bun. In fact Rosamunde's maternal grandmother was very English and very fierce, the hoodwinking French name coming from her late husband. Granny Dupont taught French in a board-ing school and often came to visit in the holidays. She was required to be addressed as 'Granny Dupont' at all times – Rachel had once experimented with 'Nanny' and her grandmother had barked at her that she was neither a goat nor a professional child minder. Needless to say, she was a firm believer in 'a stiff upper lip'.

After delivering this cruel blow and marvelling at its success (the tears had stopped entirely), Rachel flounced off to pollute the atmosphere with her Elnett hairspray as she tried to style her red curls into something approaching Diana Spencer's yuppyish blonde hairdo. She was entering the Potter's Cove Lady Di Lookalike Competition, which was taking place later that day. Even Rosamunde's best friend Kizzie, a resolute tomboy, was entering the competition, the feverish excitement of the female population of

Potter's Cove having managed to seduce even her. Only Rosamunde, it seemed, was failing to be charmed by the fairy-tale wedding. She was also fairly sure entering the competition would be pointless since her father was judging the contest and was bound to avoid any criticisms of favouritism.

Rosamunde abandoned her Sindy dolls, which Bernie had allowed to encroach on the entire landing of the Vicarage – he was a very soft touch: Granny Dupont was the fierce one. She sat herself down on the little seat tucked into the landing's bay window. It was her favourite place to sit in the whole house, with its view of Outer Cove below. She could also be nosy and see who was walking past the cottage along the path into the village. Usually she recognised every single person who walked by, but it was the height of summer and there were lots of new faces. It was thus, spying out of the landing window with her thumb firmly in her mouth, that she spotted a boy of around her own age wandering along on his own, kicking at the gravel on the path. A boy who looked bored and like he might not be too interested in the Royal Wedding either. Abandoning the window seat, Sindys forgotten, Rosamunde ran downstairs, pulled on her jelly shoes and jogged down the hilly pathway.

'Wait!' Rosamunde shouted as she approached him down the hill, unusually brave. Startled, the boy turned round and, as it became clear this strange girl with long red hair wasn't going to stop before flying into the gorse bushes ahead, he held out his arms and she tumbled into them. She looked up, then, into his eyes and saw immediately, in a way she couldn't entirely comprehend at the age of ten, that he was *someone*. His name was Stephen Jameson.

3.

MONDAY 17TH NOVEMBER 2014

'Rosie! Rosamunde darling!'

Awakened from a deep, dream-filled slumber, Rosamunde tried to summon up the energy to reply to her father, but found herself drifting back to sleep until she was stirred again by a rap at the door.

'Here, I've brought you up a cup of tea. Strong and orange, just as you like it.' Rosamunde shifted herself up onto the squashy goose-down pillows and took a grateful gulp. There was nothing like that first sip of tea in the morning. The tea she'd drunk in various corners of the globe over the last fifteen years had never tasted the same as a homely mug of Tetley.

'I'm sorry to wake you but I've got to head over to the school to take assembly this morning and I'm afraid I may not be back exactly in time for the nativity auditions. The candidates are due to arrive at ten o'clock. Would you mind terribly letting them in and giving them a cup of something?'

'Of course not, Dad,' Rosamunde replied. She took another slurp. 'But since when did you conduct auditions for the church nativity play?'

'Oh, things have changed enormously. Nowadays everyone in the village fancies themselves as the next big thing. I think it might have something to do with all the talent shows on the television. Anyway, it's become very competitive.'

'So who are we auditioning for this morning?'

'Joseph and Mary. Next week we've got the shepherds and kings. We do Jesus a little nearer the time for authenticity. Now, I must head off . . .'

'Hang on, though,' Rosamunde called as Bernie began to make his way out of the bedroom, ducking his head at the doorframe. 'What are their names?'

'Mick and Jensy – you know, they run the newsagent's – and Alison and Richard Thacker. You don't know them but they're lovely. Live in the Dickensons' old house. Must dash.' A moment later Bernie's head appeared again around the bedroom door. 'Oh, one other couple. Florence and Anna. Super girls.' And with that Bernie was gone. Rosamunde took another gulp of tea and smiled to herself. She'd forgotten what Vicarage life was like.

৩৯

Just over an hour later Rosamunde welcomed the three couples into the Vicarage. She immediately warmed to Richard Thacker, who seemed like enormous fun, and his wife Alison, who was very sweet and helped Rosamunde make the tea and coffee. In the larder was a newly baked coffee and walnut cake courtesy of Mrs Garfield, which Rosamunde deposited in the middle of the scrubbed kitchen table, around which the three couples now sat expectantly with what looked like scripts in front of them.

Although she was adept at it, Rosamunde had never been entirely comfortable with the social side of being a vicar's daughter – she was too shy at heart – and she was relieved when Bernie returned, his large figure and presence immediately making their small kitchen seem even more confined. Before he could rope her into the role of co-judge she grabbed her bag and keys to drive Bernie's ancient Citroën to Kizzie's house in the nearby town of Thatchley. It was time to catch up with her oldest friend.

∽

The house was in a modern estate but inside it was as cosy as Kizzie's old family farmhouse in Potter's Cove. There was no log fire – a gas one glowed instead – but there were books piled in every direction, small lamps burned in the corners of the sitting room, and there were Christmas carols on the CD player. Rosamunde smiled to her-self as she remembered how Kizzie had always been eager to start the festivities of Christmas. To cap it all, the delicious scent of baking mince pies pervaded the small house, the familiar but exotic smell making Rosamunde's mouth water as soon as she stepped inside.

'Rosamunde, look at you! So bloody gorgeous! So bloody tanned! Oh, it's so good to see you. Long distance phone calls just don't cut it.' Kizzie immediately clasped her friend to her ample bosom. It was a tearful reunion on both parts and Kizzie's baby soon joined in.

'Hello, little one,' said Rosamunde as she ruffled the infant's fluffy hair. 'You must be Emma,' she smiled, and the baby raised a plump hand to Rosamunde's face, calmer now. 'She's adorable,' Rosamunde told her friend.

'Most of the time,' grinned Kizzie. 'But she needs her nap. Let me put her up and you make yourself at home. I'll not be five minutes.'

Rosamunde was instantly drawn to the photos displayed on a small table behind the sofa. There was a picture of Kizzie and Gerard on their wedding day twenty years ago, at which Rosamunde had been bridesmaid. Her small friend had looked so beautiful – despite the enormous meringue-like dress – with her dark hair cascading down her back and her warm eyes gazing at Gerard. He was the strong silent type, a man whom Rosamunde had rarely witnessed utter a word but who'd clearly held an enormous appeal for Kizzie since they were in their first year of secondary school. Gerard was possibly a little too silent in Rosamunde's view, but the relationship certainly seemed to work, perhaps assisted by his long absences at sea as a fisherman.

There was also a photo of Rosamunde and Kizzie in their twenties wearing scanty summer clothes, the pair a study in contrasts with Rosamunde's dark red hair, amber eyes and tanned skin next to Kizzie with her dark-as-tar hair, fair skin and those soulful, deep brown eyes. In the photo they were laughing at something someone – the photographer, probably – had said and their eyes glittered with joy. Next to this photo was a picture of Kizzie's five children: the twins, Georgiana and Elizabeth, at nineteen, Lydia, who was sixteen, and the little ones – Harriet, who was four, and nine-month-old Emma. Kizzie had always been a huge devotee of Jane Austen.

Kizzie's life was completely alien to Rosamunde and a part of her ached at what might have been if things had turned out differently. But they hadn't, so Rosamunde, ever pragmatic, parcelled away any latent pangs.

When Kizzie returned downstairs she prepared an impromptu lunch for them both and the friends sat at the kitchen counter with a bottle of wine, trying to cram the last fifteen years into a few short hours. In tacit agreement neither referred to the events before Rosamunde had made her departure, but they eagerly discussed the news they hadn't managed to pack into their emails. Rosamunde discovered Kizzie had taken a year's maternity leave from teaching at the local primary school to focus on baby Emma, but that she'd be returning in three months' time, much to the pupils' delight – Kizzie was by far the most popular teacher, having introduced extreme sports to the PE curriculum.

'But enough about me,' she announced. 'Tell me about your travels properly,' Kizzie told her friend. 'I've been so jealous,' she added, popping an olive into her mouth. 'Where was your favourite place?'

'Oh gosh.' Rosamunde rested her chin in her hand and thought about her travels. She'd gone from country to country like a nomad, finding work or voluntary posts as she went – always ready to move on, always hoping to forget.

'Australia. Western Australia. Which is why I ended up spending my last two years there.'

'Oh, I can imagine – the beaches, the weather . . .'

'. . . the men,' finished Rosamunde, and the two women began to giggle as they'd always done at the smallest of prompts, tears running down their cheeks as they mopped hopelessly at their faces with kitchen roll, screeching until Emma woke up and put a stop to the hilarity.

'But seriously,' Kizzie continued, after Emma had been calmed and soothed. 'Has there been anyone serious since, you know . . .' She left his name hanging. Her sweetly featured face was etched with concern. Rosamunde told her about Troy, a toy boy she'd had a fling with in Perth.

'But I've enjoyed quite a few dalliances. I take lovers nowadays, you know,' Rosamunde laughed. She checked her watch before downing a black coffee and starting to gather her belongings. 'Well, I did, at least. I'm not expecting a lot of Potter's Cove.'

'Well, you're right there,' Kizzie smiled. 'I'm glad I bagged the only decent man produced by the village when I did,' she laughed. 'You'll visit again soon?' she asked as she hugged Rosamunde goodbye.

'Of course. Oh, and tell me before I go, how are your family? I haven't asked.'

'Mum and Dad are well, thanks, and Benedict is Benedict! Hopeless!' Kizzie rolled her eyes at the thought of her younger brother, who'd been the source of much irritation to her and Rosamunde throughout their childhood. 'And still gay,' she added, with a wry smile. Benedict had emerged from the closet only relatively recently. 'He's working at The Dragon's Head at the moment,' Kizzie continued. 'Drop in there sometime. He'd like to see you.'

Rosamunde nodded, though she was fairly sure she wouldn't. And for now, she needed to return to the Vicarage and find out how the auditions had gone.

જે

Letting herself in through the back door she found the kitchen pristine, with only a small lamp beside the Aga shedding any light on the room. She heard laughter coming from the sitting room. After helping a seemingly hungry Gladys to some food (the cat was a convincing liar, having been fed by Bernie only half an hour before), Rosamunde made her way to the sitting room where she found her father and Mrs Garfield chattering away beside the fire, drinking gin and tonics. It was only late afternoon but Bernie generally took the view that the sun was always over the yardarm in some part of the world, and Mrs G was not one to worry about drinking on the job.

'Rosie! There you are! I was just filling Mrs Garfield in on today's auditions. Mrs G is doubting my choice.'

'Why?' asked Rosamunde as she crouched by the fireplace, warming her cold hands in front of the blazing fire.

'Tell her who you've chosen,' Mrs Garfield ordered Bernie.

'Well, I went for Florence and Anna in the end. It was a tough call but I decided, all things being equal, that they were the best for the job,' he announced. 'You have to change with the times, Rosamunde,' he added.

'But, Dad, Joseph and Mary were clearly male and female! You can't just make them the same sex all these centuries later!' Rosamunde giggled.

'Well, I don't see that it matters,' he said. 'After all, it *was* an immaculate conception.' Bernie's lips twitched and a moment later the three of them were collapsed in hysteria. It was the second time that day that Rosamunde had needed to mop her eyes from tears of laughter, and she couldn't help but think how different it was to fifteen years ago.

4.
AUGUST 1983

'All set?'

Rosamunde looked up from her backpack to see her dad in the doorway to her bedroom. She nodded, stuffing the final item into her bag – her oldest teddy, Nibbles.

'Sure you're not missing anything? A bedtime story, perhaps?'

Rosamunde grinned up at her father. She was far too old for bedtime stories at the age of twelve and both she and her dad knew it, yet neither was ready to give them up just yet.

'Yes, I'm definitely missing that,' she said, hopping up onto her bed and patting the garishly pink duvet. Bernie squashed up next to her.

'Thought you might be. Well, it's only three o'clock in the afternoon but you'll just have to have it early, before you set off. Then you'll sleep well in the tent tonight. Budge over a little – that's right. So, what's it to be?' he asked, though he knew what she would say.

'Tell me the story about the man with the red hair and the beautiful lady.'

'All right then. Well, let me see. Once upon a time there was a young man. He was very plain in every way apart from his hair, which was brilliantly red and made him stand out even when he didn't want to. He wasn't sure what to do with his life but he was good with numbers so he decided to work in a bank. It was a good job and the money was excellent but every day was the same and he felt as though he were living in a world where everything was grey.'

Rosamunde leant against her father's shoulder, thumb in mouth, relishing every word.

'Then one day he was sitting on the lavatory when he was visited by God. He wasn't a religious man and so he was astonished. But he soon realised he was being told by God to work for him instead of the bank. So he decided to leave his sensible, well-paid job and train as a vicar. Colour began to emerge at last and yet, still, everything was a dark, muted kind of shade. Then one day the man was enjoying a pint of ale in a pub near his college when the most beautiful girl he'd ever seen walked in. He couldn't keep his eyes off her, which was not surprising. But what *was* astounding was that she couldn't keep her eyes off *him*. It wasn't long until the man married the beautiful lady and on that day, suddenly, the man's world was filled with every colour in the rainbow, the most brilliant and sparkling colours the man had ever seen.'

'He didn't ever love anyone else, did he, even when the lady died?' asked Rosamunde, as she always did.

'Only their beautiful children,' came the expected reply. 'He couldn't ever love another woman because a man can only hope to experience love like that once in a lifetime,' Bernie finished. 'Now, my darling girl,' he said, ruffling Rosamunde's hair. 'It's time you were off.'

'I love that story,' sighed Rosamunde.

'I know you do.'

❧

Safely ensconced in a cosy sleeping bag in the tent she was sharing with Kizzie and Rachel, Rosamunde awoke the next day to the delicious scents of dew-drenched canvas and cooking sausages. It was the annual weekend camp laid on for local children by Kizzie's parents in one of the fields on their farm and without a doubt the highlight of Rosamunde's year. There was something so pleasingly simple about camping and it always gave her the giggles, especially late at night when they were meant to be going to sleep. Rachel had resorted to stuffing tissues in her mouth last night, which had only prolonged her hysteria.

After pulling on wellies over her pink pyjamas, Rosamunde unzipped her way out of the tent and headed straight to the camp-fire, guided by her hungry belly. Rachel and Kizzie were reluctant to emerge from their sleeping bags and she was keen to find Stephen and make sure she was included in whatever plans he had for the day. She had now known Stephen for two years and had begun to develop something of a crush. She wasn't the only one. Stephen had a sort of magnetism – partly due to his character and perhaps also to his transience, as he only came to Potter's Cove for the summer holidays, to stay with his grandmother. He was always included in local events and was incredibly popular. Even Rachel failed to be disdainful about him. He was taller than most chil-dren his age and had cropped blond hair, amused turquoise eyes and a confident way about him that made him seem older than his peers.

'Morning, trouble.' He grinned his dimpled smile at Rosamunde as she perched down next to him on one of the logs arranged by Kizzie's mother around the campfire. She quietly relished the prospect of a few moments alone with him, knowing that at any moment his other disciples would appear sleepily from the tents scattered around the dewy field.

'What's the plan today?' Rosamunde asked, trying to sound nonchalant but suspecting she sounded too eager, as usual.

'There's activities on this afternoon. Swimming races and stuff down at the beach. But this morning we're free to do whatever we want. Let's have breakfast then head up to the cliffs,' he announced.

'Okay,' Rosamunde agreed, helping herself to a deliciously burnt sausage and a mug of strong tea. After scoffing breakfast she told Stephen she'd get dressed and rally Kizzie and Rachel.

'I thought we might head off just us two,' he suggested, shrugging. Rosamunde couldn't believe her luck, but was a little unsure.

'But I'll need to get dressed and then they'll want to come.'

'So come in your pyjamas. They look like a tracksuit anyway. Come on,' he said, standing up. Stephen was already dressed in drainpipe jeans, plimsolls and a tight black t-shirt that made him look like John Travolta in *Grease*. Rosamunde only wished she looked more like Olivia Newton-John. She was still uncertain but then she spotted Benedict poking his head out of a nearby tent and the last thing she wanted was for him to join them, so she shrugged too in agreement. After quickly promising Kizzie's mother to stick together and return by lunchtime, they left their comrades behind and began the steep climb to the cliffs.

It was a beautiful day: sunny but not too hot. There was a whispery breeze that lifted Rosamunde's thick hair off her back as she trudged up the steps that led from Potter's Cove to the cliffs, and the smell of coconut oozed from the bright yellow gorse bushes. Stephen walked quickly and seemed barely out of breath when they reached the top, whilst Rosamunde was fairly sure her face had turned an unattractive shade of beetroot. She was unsure why she had suddenly become so aware of her appearance, having barely given it a second thought until recently. Perhaps Rachel's obsession with her looks (and, frankly, herself in general) was rubbing off on her. She hoped not.

At the top Stephen turned around and waited patiently for Rosamunde to catch up.

'Can I ask you a question?' Stephen asked as she approached. He didn't wait for Rosamunde to answer one way or another. 'How come you and your sister both have red hair and sort of yellow eyes but your sister has really pale skin and yours is suntanned?'

Rosamunde was taken aback. She'd never noticed the difference in their complexions, although now she thought about it, Rachel did have to be much more careful to stay out of the sun. Rosamunde was quiet for a moment, thinking. Stephen grinned.

'What?' Rosamunde asked, noticing his smile.

'Oh, it's just I love the way you never rush to answer a question. You really think about things before you answer. It's unusual.'

Rosamunde was unsure if this was a good thing or not but she continued to consider quietly. They walked along side by side as she did so.

'I think it's because my mum was half French,' she announced finally. 'She had dark hair and skin that went really brown, like a nut. Rachel and I both inherited Dad's hair and eyes but I guess I got Mum's skin and Rachel got Dad's.'

Stephen seemed satisfied with this answer. 'What happened to your mum? Gran said she died but she didn't know how.'

Rosamunde felt her chest begin to feel sore. It always happened when she thought too much about her mother. She hoped she wouldn't start crying. She bit her lip and answered quickly.

'She died of a brain tumour five years ago. It all happened really suddenly. She used to say our eyes were a colour called amber, not yellow. It's hard . . .' She faltered.

'I know,' Stephen said quietly and he seemed all at once less self-assured.

'You do?' asked Rosamunde, tentatively. An atmosphere of sadness seemed to crackle between them.

'I had a sister, only a year older than me. We were as close as twins. She died too. Of meningitis. It happened five years ago, the same as you,' he explained, his skin reddening with emotion.

'That's so awful,' Rosamunde told him.

'No worse than what happened to you,' replied Stephen. 'And in some strange way it's made me stronger. I feel older, somehow, and like I've got to be brave for my mum and dad. I used to shelter behind Claire a lot, but now I have to be strong. Confident, like Claire always was.'

'You're like my sister,' said Rosamunde. 'She's been so amazing since Mum died. I wish I could be like that. I just feel sad and pathetic.'

'You're not that. You're braver than you think. Sometimes, you know, it's braver to cry,' he said, noticing suddenly the tears in Rosamunde's eyes. He said nothing more but slowly, tentatively, he took her hand. As they continued along the cliff path they remained hand in hand until the path began to narrow and it became difficult to walk together any longer. When Stephen let go Rosamunde could still feel a comforting, buzzing warmth in the palm of that hand.

5.

SATURDAY 22ND NOVEMBER 2014

Rosamunde woke with a start, her heart hammering. She checked her watch. It was two o'clock in the morning and yet the house telephone was ringing, shrill and persistent. She clambered out of bed and found her dressing gown, tying the satin belt around her waist whilst poking her feet into her slippers. By the time she reached the downstairs hallway she found her father, bleary-eyed in striped pyjamas, picking up the receiver.

'Vicarage,' he said, in automatic fashion. Rosamunde settled on the stairs, inquisitive. She could only hear her father's side of the conversation but it was clear the news was not good.

'Oh my dear,' he said. 'You did well to ring me. Now, have you called the doctor? Yes. Deep breaths now. Okay, now listen, my dear. I'm coming right round. Make sure the door's unlocked and I'll let myself in. I'll be there in just a tick.'

Having replaced the receiver, Bernie looked up at Rosamunde. He appeared both calm and sad, she thought.

'What's happened?' she asked. By now she was wide awake, adrenalin coursing through her veins.

'That was poor Alison Thacker. It sounds as though Richard's had a heart attack. Alison went to bed while he watched the golf but when she woke up to find he hadn't come to bed she went downstairs and found him slumped in the armchair, dead as a dodo. So terribly, terribly young. He can't have been a day over forty-five,' he mused, rubbing his white head. 'I must get over there now,' he added, moving swiftly past Rosamunde up the stairs.

'Can I help at all?' called Rosamunde after him. She felt rather useless.

'No, my darling. You go back to bed. Just feed Gladys for me if I'm not back for a while.'

He left a few minutes later, having dressed haphazardly and brushed his teeth. Rosamunde returned to bed but couldn't sleep. She kept thinking about the couple, who'd been auditioning for the roles of Joseph and Mary in this very house just a few days ago. She tossed and turned until the sky turned from black to dark blue and she decided to give in and head downstairs to put the kettle on.

Later that morning Bernie ushered Alison into the house and straight to his study. Rosamunde brought them tea and biscuits, which she discreetly deposited on Bernie's desk, pausing for a moment before shutting the door. She could hear her father's soothing tones as he calmed the woman who'd lost her husband and who had no children to console or distract her. Rosamunde was reminded of the serious side of her father's job and how good he was at it. Eccentric and full of fun he might be, but in times of crisis Bernie was the perfect combination of soothing and comforting, practical and pragmatic.

∾

It was now the afternoon and, having delivered Alison into the capable hands of her mother, Bernie was off duty. He and Rosamunde sprawled themselves on a sofa each in the sitting room to watch the afternoon's rugby match on the television while

Gladys, with her large, graceful body and distinctly ginger hue, stretched smugly across the hearth-rug. She knew she had the best position in the room.

After celebrating England's win over Samoa, Rosamunde and her father were debating over what to watch. Bernie liked the look of *The X Factor* and, although Rosamunde thought she'd prefer *Strictly Come Dancing*, when she saw Bernie's tired face she decided graciously to concede defeat.

She thought it would be easier to eat dinner from trays on their laps and so, as Bernie sipped red wine and chuckled at *The X Factor*, Rosamunde went through to the kitchen to prepare a simple supper of soup with hunks of farmhouse loaf.

She loved the kitchen in winter with its homely red Aga, oozing warmth and comfort, and the ancient pine table tucked into the corner, around which there was just enough room for six chairs. Bernie's large chair sat at the head of the table and behind this could be found the walk-in larder. Rosamunde drew the red and white gingham curtains, shutting out the dark night. She'd always hated the thought that snoopers might easily observe her from outside as she pottered about, though she recognised this was somewhat fanciful as Potter's Cove wasn't known for its crime rate.

To the other side of the Aga was a droopy old chair, covered in cat hair, which was mainly used for depositing coats, hats and scarves, since it was near the back door, and to the left of this door were the kitchen units, which were made of wood and painted cream. Rosamunde liked how unfussy they were. She also loved the fact that the sink was just beneath the window and enjoyed far-reaching sea views, with the result that any washing-up that needed to be done was hardly a chore.

She found a dark blue pan, reassuringly housed in the cupboard that had always contained saucepans, and set about heating the soup. While it simmered, she found a breadboard and knife and cut the loaf, and when all was ready she carefully loaded the food onto a tray and took it through to the sitting room.

After the viewing and eating were over, Rosamunde and Bernie chatted as they polished off the remainder of the wine. It was their usual sort of conversation – general chit-chat, nothing too serious. But then Bernie shuffled on the sofa a little. He cleared his throat. Rosamunde knew what was coming.

'We haven't really talked about things, have we?' he asked, topping up both glasses. He always kept the bottle within arm's reach.

'What things?' Rosamunde asked, deliberately obstructive, buying herself time.

'Oh, Rosie,' he said sadly. 'You were such an open little girl. So emotional and sensitive. I always knew what you were feeling. You were quiet as you are now – well, compared to your sister – and always considered, but so honest about your feelings. Now you're such a closed book. If somebody asked me if you were happy, I wouldn't know. I really wouldn't.' He raised his kindly eyes to her, pleading for something. He paused. 'Are you happy?'

Rosamunde considered the question. She wasn't unhappy. Not like she was before. As time had passed she'd become accepting.

'I'm contented,' she told her father eventually. 'I was dreadfully unhappy back then, with everything that happened. But it was good for me to get away. I was able to see the world, to put my own problems into perspective, to meet people without establishing any lasting connections. I needed it. But in the end I missed it here terribly and I started to have these dreams . . .' She tailed off. 'I suddenly realised it was time to return home for good. Anyway, there was this man. Troy. The relationship had run its course,' Rosamunde explained.

'And now? Have you thought about the future? You're only just forty-four, Rosie. You're young. You can't hole yourself up with me in this tiny village for the rest of your life.'

'I just want to be peaceful, Dad. No dramas, no love affairs. I'm quite content to be on my own now, with no one to please but myself. I'll find a little job, nothing too demanding. Thankfully I managed to make a bit of money working for that mining company towards the end of my time in Australia so I'm in no major hurry. And I'm not going to think about the future right now. If there's one thing I learnt when I was away it was to live in the present.'

Bernie was sad for his daughter but understood. And he seemed to know she'd opened up enough for one evening.

'Well, I know you're not thinking ahead but have you decided when you're going to visit Rachel? She's absolutely itching to see you.'

Rosamunde drained her glass and smiled at the thought of seeing her sister.

'Monday,' she decided aloud. 'On Monday I shall take a train to London . . .'

'. . . to visit the Queen,' Bernie finished, and they laughed at their old joke, first started by Marguerite when the girls were small and any visit to London involved a trip to Buckingham Palace.

An hour later, curled snugly in her bed, Rosamunde listened to the wind wrangling with the trees outside her window and wriggled her toes under the duvet with the sheer joy of being tucked up in bed on a winter's night in her childhood home. *Not exactly happy*, she thought as she drifted into sleep. *But definitely content.* Gladys purred in agreement.

6.

JULY 1985

It was the summer holidays and it had done nothing but rain so far. Rosamunde was fourteen and at that horrible cusp between childhood and adolescence. Her body was galloping into adolescent territory – puppy fat, developing breasts and some angry red spots on her neck – but she was in no way ready to relinquish the benefits of childhood. Luckily for her Kizzie was in no hurry to grow up either and had recently devised a club that would satisfy her urge for adventure, appropriately named Tough Club.

Kizzie and Rosamunde were the only proper members, though other individuals were intermittently invited to join in – principally when a game required more than two people to be interesting – but the pair were very choosy, or as choosy as they could be: their 'guest member' was usually Benedict. Rosamunde wasn't half as intrepid as Kizzie; in fact, she felt quite wimpy by comparison, but then Kizzie *was* remarkably fearless. The Club involved daily meetings, at which they began proceedings by singing their Tough Club anthem, followed by whatever game or assault course had been devised for the day. By the time they were two weeks into the summer holidays, Kizzie's assault courses were bordering on lunacy and Rosamunde had ripped two pairs of jeans.

'Can we do something other than an assault course today?' Rosamunde asked her friend, as they sat at the landing window of the Vicarage watching the rain clattering down outside. Rosamunde was picking at the latest hole in her jeans and her whole body felt bruised and achy from the adventures of the last couple of weeks. Kizzie's eyes were bright, her creative mind ready for a new challenge.

'Okay,' she agreed. 'In fact, I have just the thing in mind. Come on,' she beckoned bossily, and Rosamunde followed her downstairs where they pulled on their wellies and headed out into the village.

Kizzie, though adventurous, was naturally sweet-natured and generally a rule abider, so Rosamunde was stunned when her friend told her what game she had in mind – 'knock knock ginger'! Rosamunde had played the game before with Rachel, who was anything but rule abiding, and she had to admit it had been fun, if a little nerve-wracking. The girls decided to let Benedict join in with this particular game, so they found him down at Inner Cove and let him in on their plans.

There was a square of thatched cottages not far from the beach, with a little path leading away from them, and they decided on this for their venue. The first house they chose clearly had no one inside, so they started with this as a practice run. They took it in turns to knock loudly on the front door before scurrying, giggling, along the damp path that led back to the beach, then returning for another go.

Having mustered up more courage, the trio then decided on another cottage where they could see a man sitting on his sofa, watching television. He was perfectly positioned, his back to the rain-spattered window.

'You go first,' whispered Kizzie to Rosamunde, and she bravely crept up to the front door, knocked twice and scuttled back to Kizzie and Benedict. The three of them ran swiftly along the pathway until they were safely out of sight.

'Do you think he answered the door?' asked Rosamunde, out of breath, her cheeks rosy with exertion.

'Next time we'll stop behind that oak tree over there so we can see if he answers,' ordered Kizzie and they all agreed. This time it was Kizzie's turn. As soon as she'd knocked the three ran behind the tree and waited breathlessly. A grumpy-looking man of about fifty soon opened the door. He stepped outside and looked left and right before shaking his head, muttering and returning inside. Giggles came from behind the tree.

'Your turn now, Benedict,' said Kizzie. 'And this time we'll run down the path again.' Looking nervous, Benedict approached the front door. He knocked loudly four times yet on the fourth, as he was poised to run away, the door opened. He froze for a brief moment before turning on his welly heel and sprinting down the path, with Rosamunde and Kizzie following behind. Benedict was speedy and soon sprinted out of reach, but before the girls knew it the man had hold of their ponytails and they were forced to come to an abrupt halt.

'You menacing little kids!' the man shouted at them. Rosamunde's legs began to wobble with fear and a trickle of rain ran down her forehead into her left eye. She rubbed at it.

'And a vicar's daughter too!' remarked the man, recognising Rosamunde from the village. 'I'll be having words with your father,' he told her. 'But not until I've called the police,' he added threateningly, and with that he released his grip on the girls' hair and they staggered off, lightheaded with shock.

'Why did Benedict have to knock so many times?' muttered Kizzie as they sought safety in Rosamunde's bedroom back at the Vicarage.

'Typical,' said Rosamunde. It was perhaps a little unfair on Benedict, but this wasn't the first time he'd ruined one of their games. Nor, they suspected, would it be the last.

For the next few days the girls – and to a lesser degree Benedict – lived in fear of the police turning up at their houses, and of the scolding they'd receive when their parents found out. In the end Rosamunde confessed all to Bernie, who gave her a cursory telling-off whilst looking vaguely amused, but it seemed the man had decided against reporting the girls, though he'd certainly made them sweat and – in Rosamunde's case – confess. Tough Club had now slightly lost its appeal. But soon enough Rosamunde had a new distraction: the arrival of Stephen in Potter's Cove for the rest of the summer holidays. He was arriving later than normal this year, having been in Portugal with his parents.

❧

It was the end of July and Stephen had thankfully brought summer with him. Finally the rain had stopped and the sun cheered everyone. Not only that, but on the same day Stephen arrived, the annual travelling fair had also pitched up in Thatchley. Rosamunde looked forward to the arrival of the fair every year, and this one was no exception. She was terrified by most of the rides but there was an atmosphere to the whole event that made her feel wonderfully alive.

On the first night, Bernie dropped Rachel and Rosamunde off, and as soon as they entered the fairground Rosamunde inhaled the distinctive scents of candyfloss and danger that mingled with the coconut aroma of sun lotion still lingering on her skin.

Rachel immediately began to flirt with one of the fairground workers whilst Rosamunde went in search of her friends. She located them by the dodgems: Kizzie, Benedict, Stephen and Clara Johnson. They were bound to be joined by other friends later, making it even harder to compete for Stephen's interest, but for now Rosamunde hoped she would be able to bask in a little of his attention. She had new competition, however. It seemed Clara, one of Benedict's contemporaries, was also taken with Stephen, who was looking more gorgeous than ever with his Portuguese suntan and sun-bleached hair. Clara was only eleven but seemed much older than that physically – she was a big, tall girl. Emotionally, however, she could be immature and spiteful. She was also fearless, bold enough to pick a fight with any older kids who might stand in her way.

'Hi, Rosamunde,' Stephen said, untangling himself from Clara who was stuck to him like glue. 'How's it going?' he asked.

'Fine, thanks,' was Rosamunde's uninspired reply as she blushed deeply.

'Anyone up for a go on the dodgems while we wait for the others to turn up?' suggested Stephen.

They all agreed – of course – and clambered up onto the podium. The music was deafening but as soon as the last ride had come to a standstill the group claimed their cars. Clara cleverly managed to hop into a dodgem with Stephen and Rachel re-emerged and grabbed hold of Kizzie, which left Rosamunde to share a dodgem with Benedict, much to her annoyance. The next thing she knew they were being battered about all over the place as the music blared. Rosamunde thought her head might fall off but she was soon screaming with delight. As soon as the ride stopped they weaved their way out and Benedict promptly threw up all over Rosamunde's new pumps.

'Oh dear!' said Rachel, inadequately, before swiftly suggesting heading to the candyfloss stand. Benedict looked quite green at the prospect. Kizzie put an arm around him and led him to the kiosk, where Stephen offered to place the order while the others hung around waiting. Rosamunde looked down at the sick on her shoes and started to feel queasy herself. Rachel could have her candyfloss.

'You do realise you have no chance with Stephen, don't you?' Clara was suddenly standing directly in front of Rosamunde.

'What . . . what do you mean?' stammered Rosamunde.

'Oh, come on,' replied Clara, her voice as whiney as always. 'It's so obvious you fancy him, but he's way out of your league. Look at you. Chubby, spotty and – even worse – ginger. He wouldn't go out with you if you were the last girl on the planet,' Clara finished triumphantly. Rosamunde felt her face redden and tears spring to her eyes. She was mortified. If Clara realised she fancied Stephen, it must be clear to everyone – including him. She couldn't bear the thought of them all laughing at her behind her back. She turned and ran off to the portaloos, where she locked herself in and, after rinsing her shoes, sat down on the latrine and tried to compose herself. After five minutes there was a knock on the door.

'Rosamunde? Are you in there?' It was Kizzie.

'Just coming,' Rosamunde replied, rubbing her eyes.

'Hurry up! Everyone's waiting. We're going on the ghost train. You okay?' she asked with concern when she saw Rosamunde's watery eyes.

'Just something in my eye, a piece of grit or something,' Rosamunde lied. She didn't want to put a damper on things for everyone else, even if she was churning up inside.

This time, as chance would have it, Rosamunde was next to Stephen on the ride. Admittedly she had Benedict on her left again and hoped he'd got over his nausea, but she was prepared to put up with him for the opportunity of having Stephen nestled so closely on her right. The ride began and soon the trio were being freaked out by spooky noises and creepy hands crawling through their hair and down their backs. Here and there they came face to face with a skeleton or a bat but just as the ride had almost reached its big-fright ending, Rosamunde felt another sensation: a sweet, dry kiss on her right cheek.

Stephen didn't say a word and he didn't look at her when they emerged into the evening sunlight, but Rosamunde found her downcast mood lifting at once, her spirits rising high. She looked over at Clara, who'd been wedged between David and Paul Pendrick – two very unappealing brothers – and noticed she was giving her daggers. It was so tempting to march over to Clara and tell her what had just happened, but Rosamunde decided to be silently triumphant. And in any case, it was her secret. Hers and Stephen's. As she left the fairground with Rachel to meet their father she looked back over her shoulder at Stephen. He looked straight back at her and winked.

7.
SUNDAY 23RD NOVEMBER 2014

It was a busy day for Bernie. He'd had his normal communion service in the morning and in the afternoon was required to conduct a carol service at the old people's home in Thatchley. It was still November but the old folk liked to get into the spirit of Christmas nice and early. Rosamunde remembered attending with her father years ago and chattering to the pensioners, so she decided to go along with him again today, much to Bernie's delight. He had no problem with the whole event but he was a little terrified of Matron and, as soon as they arrived, Rosamunde could see why.

'Hello, Vicar,' drawled a glamour-puss lady of a certain age as she made to straighten Bernie's dog collar with her scarlet-painted talons. Matron was tall and slim with a very pert bosom that she thrust towards Bernie in an exceedingly inviting fashion. He looked scared stiff.

'It's such a joy to see you, Vicar,' Matron continued, coquettishly flapping her false eyelashes. Her lips were painted a juicy red and her dyed dark hair had been coiffed into a very stiff-looking bouffant. She'd clearly made some effort.

'Thank you,' Bernie mumbled. 'Now, is everything set up for the service?' he asked, trying desperately to be businesslike in the face of her obvious flirtation. Rosamunde was highly amused.

'We're all ready for you, Vicar,' Matron smiled suggestively. She had managed to ignore Rosamunde up until this point but she did now glance at her and point in the direction of some stainless steel tea urns and an array of china teacups.

'The tea's all ready for after the service,' she told Rosamunde briskly. 'You can offer it round,' she ordered before clapping her hands loudly.

They had arrived in the day room, which was like a hothouse but without the pleasant scent of exotic flowers. Instead it smelt sadly of old age and institutional dinners. Rosamunde took off her jacket and cardigan and still felt too hot. Bernie – in his cassock – had gone rather puce, though Rosamunde wasn't sure if this was from the heat or his embarrassment.

'Quieten down, everyone,' ordered Matron, though the dear old ladies and gents seated around the room had hardly been making a sound. Somebody switched off the television.

'I was watching that,' complained an old man with no teeth.

'Well, we have a lovely treat for you, Arthur,' Matron told him. 'The vicar is here to conduct a Christmas carol service for you all. Now isn't that super?' A couple of the old dears nodded.

'Bernie will be starting with some prayers and a reading, and then we'll have a couple of carols. Mavis, you've been practising them on the piano, haven't you, dear? Can you remember the ones we're going to sing?' Mavis nodded obligingly.

She was a spry-looking lady – just like a little sparrow, especially when she cocked her head to the side to listen to Bernie.

Without further ado, Bernie started the service with prayers and a reading and, soon enough, Mavis struck up the familiar tune

41

of *Hark the Herald Angels Sing* followed by *The Holly and the Ivy*. The residents' spirits seemed to be lifted by the sing-along and as Rosamunde offered around tea and biscuits the atmosphere had become really quite jolly. But all of a sudden, as she served another cup of tea to an elderly lady, she found herself being pinched on the bottom. She squeaked and looked round to find an old gent smiling at her lasciviously. She could barely believe it.

Having witnessed this incident with some surprise, Bernie made his excuses to Matron and, after some speedy goodbyes, he and Rosamunde dashed out of the old people's home. They scurried down the hill to The Three Bells, leaving the car parked outside the home, and only when they'd entered the pub did they let rip the laughter that had been bubbling up within them.

'I can't believe he pinched my bum!' exclaimed Rosamunde. 'He was at least eighty!'

'That's old Charlie Meadle!' laughed Bernie, mopping at his face with a dotty hanky. 'You know who he is, don't you?' he asked, as he managed to stop chortling long enough to order them their drinks.

'Who?' asked Rosamunde.

'He was the victim of your "knock knock ginger!" game all those years ago. Do you remember? You were so worried he was going to report you and Kizzie to the police. You confessed everything to me! I was very amused; you'd managed to pick the house of the grumpiest man in the village.'

'I can't believe it!' chuckled Rosamunde. 'Well, he finally got his revenge on me,' she marvelled. 'And you were lucky not to get your bottom pinched by Matron,' she giggled to her father.

'Don't!' he replied. 'I've never been so terrified in my life!'

Still wiping their eyes, Bernie and Rosamunde made their way to the fireside where they sat back with relief and enjoyed a well-earned drink.

'There's one thing you can say for Vicarage life,' remarked Rosamunde. 'It's never dull. I've spent the last fifteen years travelling the globe and yet somehow life at the Vicarage in Potter's Cove is still more interesting.'

'I can't tell you how lovely it is to have you home,' said Bernie, seriously, covering Rosamunde's hand with his own paper-dry paw, now gnarled with arthritis. As she felt his old hand on hers, Rosamunde felt her eyes watering again – this time with sadness. Old age comes to us all in the end, she thought, and her dear old dad had been robbed of his chance to grow old disgracefully with the love of his life. Rosamunde felt suddenly weighed down by the unfairness of it. Bernie looked at his daughter.

'Don't be sad,' he said gently, perceptive as always. 'It's all okay.' He raised his gin and tonic to her proudly.

8.
JULY 1986

It was the most promising day of the year – the start of the summer holidays – and Rosamunde grinned with anticipation as A-ha burst onto the radio beside her bed. She was completely in love with Morten Harket and had a poster of him stuck with Blu-tack to the ceiling above her bed.

Rosamunde was beyond excited, but this wasn't just down to the sense of freedom that comes at the prospect of six whole weeks without teachers breathing down your neck. Today was the day she would finally see Stephen again and this summer she was determined they would kiss. Last summer their relationship had still been very much platonic, despite Rosamunde's deepening crush, but this year would be different, she was certain. For a start, she was fifteen now and looked far more grown up. She wasn't quite in the same league as Rachel, who'd adopted the lace-gloved, peroxide-tinged persona of Madonna, which was a little full-on for Potter's Cove in Rosamunde's opinion (it was embarrassing, actually, especially in church on Sundays), but she'd lost her puppy fat entirely and was definitely developing proper cheekbones, which she highlighted with some bright pink blusher of Rachel's. Yes, all in all she was feeling much more confident.

'Rosamunde!' She was dragged harshly out of her daydreaming by the familiar bark of her grandmother. 'Rosamunde! Breakfast. Now!' Granny Dupont was a stickler for routine, even in the school holidays, so Rosamunde was rarely permitted a lie-in when her grandmother was staying with them, which was all too frequently in everyone's opinion. Rachel was eighteen and decamped to her boyfriend's house whenever Granny Dupont came to stay, but if her grandmother noticed the snub she didn't remark on it.

As Rosamunde sat at the breakfast table eating her regimented soldiers and boiled egg, there was a loud rap at the back door.

'Who on earth can it be at this hour?' asked Granny Dupont, without expecting an answer. Rosamunde was mute at this hour of the day and Bernie had his head firmly in the *Telegraph*. They sat gormlessly for a moment longer before Granny Dupont made a song and dance about getting up from the table, brushing the crumbs off her dirndl skirt, stripping off her apron and opening the door. Rosamunde was in equal parts elated and mortified for there, at eight o'clock on the first day of the summer holidays, stood Stephen.

'Sorry to call so early,' he said, smiling his confident, dimply smile at Granny Dupont. He never failed to try to charm her, though he made little headway in thawing the ice.

'I arrived late last night and Gran said the tide this morning would be perfect for taking the boat out. I just wondered if you might be interested, Rosamunde?' he asked, peeping past the bulk of Granny Dupont to Rosamunde, who was still sitting frozen at the breakfast table calculating how hideous she must look with her crumpled hair, sleepy eyes and embarrassingly childish pyjamas.

'Great!' she managed, scraping back the pine chair and backing out of the kitchen towards the stairs. 'Give me five minutes! Make yourself at home!' She didn't think there was much chance of that with Granny Dupont on the warpath, but what did he expect, turning up like this? What was wrong with the telephone? Rosamunde found herself feeling quite grumpy about being sprung upon like this when she'd planned in great detail the outfit and hairstyle she'd be sporting when she first saw Stephen this summer.

'Lover boy here, is he?'

Rosamunde glanced up from the wardrobe where she was ago-nising over what to wear for a boat trip that would be appropriate yet still look enticing.

'I thought you were at Tim's,' she snapped at her sister.

'I was. Just got back. What's with the attitude?'

'I've got five minutes to get ready – no, make that three – and no idea what to wear. We're going out on his boat. You've got to help me, Rachel! I need to make a good impression!' she pleaded.

Rachel might have opted for a dramatic style herself, but she was brilliant at choosing clothes for Rosamunde that suited her less flamboyant nature. She picked out some navy pumps, leggings and an oversized stripy t-shirt. After dabbing on a little make-up and blitzing her hair with a diffuser, Rosamunde had to admit she looked just right. Sort of nautical, yet funky.

'You're good to go!' announced Rachel. 'Have fun!' she added with a nudge. Rosamunde blushed and bounded downstairs. She planned to.

The trip was not a disappointment. It was a sultry, hazy day and the sea was as calm and unruffled as Stephen was. He guided the speedboat expertly out of the bay and into the open expanse of water ahead of them, speeding up and making Rosamunde giggle with exhilaration as she was jiggled up and down in her seat, the cool splash of sea-spray permeating itself into her outfit and hair. By the time they approached Kipper's Cove she was drenched but happy.

'Not feeling too sick?' Stephen called, as he guided the boat carefully between some rocks and hurled the anchor over the side.

'No, I'm fine!' yelled back Rosamunde.

'Good.'

A moment later Stephen was there beside Rosamunde, his attention now entirely focused on her instead of the boat. She felt herself melting inside as he stroked her cheek. She was mute, barely breathing. For a small moment she felt anxious in case she would be a hopeless kisser but very quickly she realised her fears were unfounded. Their lips locked so instinctively, and their mouths seemed so hungry for each other, that their first proper kiss seemed completely and utterly intuitive.

Though Rosamunde was naïve she knew it was natural for a kiss to develop further, but Stephen seemed entirely happy to spend the morning with their lips entwined. She was glad, for she knew it was too soon for anything else, and if he'd expected more she feared it would have spoiled the day. Instead, it was the most perfect day of her life. When their lips were red and swollen from kissing and sea-spray, Stephen produced a picnic hamper he'd prepared, crammed with deliciously simple food and two small bottles of ginger beer. There were Marmite and lettuce sandwiches, packets of Discos and some half-melted Wagon Wheels.

After stuffing themselves they lay on the deck sunbathing.

'Have you kissed many girls?' Rosamunde asked coyly, rolling onto her side towards Stephen.

'A few,' Stephen grinned. He propped himself up on his arms and looked into her amber eyes. Then suddenly he looked serious, so unlike him. 'You're different, though, Rosamunde.'

Rosamunde met his gaze, before reaching over and planting a gentle, tender kiss on Stephen's lips as if to seal a deal. They lay silently then, hand in hand, as the boat swayed lightly beneath them, until Stephen's nose began to turn pink and they took turns diving off the deck into the depths of the sea below them.

By the time they returned to land Rosamunde knew something had shifted in their relationship. Her legs were wobbling as she climbed ashore, and she knew it wasn't just the contrast between sea and land. They were trembling with love and anticipation. There was no going back.

9.

MONDAY 24TH NOVEMBER 2014

Monday morning dawned cold and dark. A howling wind was bending the willow tree towards Rosamunde's bedroom window, as if it was desperate to climb through the thin panes to the warmth of the room inside. Rosamunde wondered if she might cancel her visit to London after all and remain wrapped in the comfort of her duvet today, but she reprimanded herself for her idleness and pulled her slender feet out of bed into the cosy slippers she'd had the forethought to place within reach the night before.

Before she left, Rosamunde poked her head around the door of Bernie's study to say goodbye. He was still in pyjamas and sat in his armchair with a mug of steaming tea as he listened to Radio 4. Rosamunde loved this room. It had such an air of masculinity about it, with its aroma of dusty old books and Old Spice. The room was only small and three of the four walls were lined with books and various knick-knacks, which made it seem even cosier.

Bernie's antique desk with its dark green leather blotting pad stood proudly against the other wall and rather than having a practical, ergonomic office chair he used an old dining chair with a vicious-looking upright back. An old oak chest stood to the side of the desk and housed a radio and various family photos.

There was a bag of golf clubs in the gap between the desk and the chest, even though Bernie hadn't played for years, and fishing rods were crammed into the same gap although Rosamunde had never known her father to go fishing. He was a dreadful hoarder but it made for a room that was endlessly fascinating and a perfect tableau of Bernie's life.

༺༝༺

At Thatchley station it was still dark and soon the rain began. Slow, large drops at first, followed by an almighty downpour. Rosamunde shivered inside her velvet coat and pulled her scarf over her head for protection. She was relieved when the train for Totnes finally charged into the station and she was able to find a seat in the stuffy warmth of a remarkably full carriage. She supposed her fellow passengers were heading to Totnes or maybe on to London for a Christmas shopping excursion. The thought made her realise that, of course, she too would need to buy presents. She found an old notepad and a poorly working biro in her bag and, locating a blank page, began to make a list of the family and friends she would need to buy for.

Rosamunde was engrossed in this task when she found herself being spattered with raindrops again, as a late and out-of-breath passenger thoughtlessly shook his umbrella before squeezing himself opposite her into the only available seat remaining in the carriage. Rosamunde begrudgingly moved her handbag from the table and the man began to spread out his newspaper in another inconsiderate move. It was only after he had finally ruffled his paper into an arrangement he was satisfied with that Rosamunde saw his face.

'Benedict?' she asked, though she was not sure why, since this man was clearly Kizzie's brother – those dark curls and round, dark eyes were features he and his sibling still shared, though Benedict's hair was scattered with some flecks of white. Although Rosamunde had come across Benedict now and again in her adult years she still always thought of him as Kizzie's annoying younger brother.

'Oh. My. Goodness,' Benedict remarked as he absorbed the fact of Rosamunde's presence opposite him (*Yes, definitely gay*, Rosamunde thought). 'I can't believe it! I haven't seen you in . . .'

'. . . fifteen years,' Rosamunde finished. Benedict leaned across to embrace her, managing to knock his neighbour's polystyrene cup of tea across the table and into everyone's laps. After a great deal of mopping up with hopelessly un-absorbent napkins Benedict and Rosamunde found themselves able to catch up with each other's news, skirting around the issue of relationships as only two people renowned for being disastrous in love will do. Rosamunde discovered Benedict was now a potter by profession.

'A potter? In Potter's Cove? That's ridiculous, Benedict!' Rosamunde laughed.

'I know, it's sad, but there you go . . . I love it here, I don't want to move, and I love my job too. So I guess I'm stuck being the cliché of a potter in Potter's Cove for now. Although, to be frank, I've lost my motivation at the moment. That's why I'm working in The Dragon's Head. When I split up with Clara she managed to take my creative inspiration with her.'

Rosamunde understood that Benedict had finished with Clara after realising he was 'batting for the other team', as Bernie would say. Rosamunde knew she should feel sympathy towards poor Clara, who'd been planning their wedding virtually since they were children. They were a couple for many years before Benedict's sudden realisation three years ago; Rosamunde had been amazed to read of such a dramatic story as she'd checked her emails at a sweaty cyber-café in Bali.

The trouble was that Clara had been a source of even greater irritation than Benedict when Rosamunde was growing up. As a small child she was simply whingey and unimaginative (Rosamunde and Kizzie always had to invent the games they played), but as she'd got older she'd become bitchy and backstabbing, traits that had accompanied her into adulthood. She'd never managed to shake off the whiney voice either. All in all, Rosamunde felt Benedict had been granted a lucky escape.

Despite the less than promising beginning to their encounter, Rosamunde found herself slightly disappointed when they reached Totnes and were required to go their separate ways; Benedict was indeed going Christmas shopping and Totnes was as far as he was prepared to venture on this miserable November day. Rosamunde was forced to admit he had become a lot more appealing over the years. He was still a little bumbling and clumsy, but she hadn't realised how amusing he was until now. And he'd somehow grown more comfortable in his own skin, perhaps down to finally acknowledging his sexuality. As a result he was really rather good company.

Rosamunde was hoping they would have an opportunity to meet up back in Potter's Cove when Benedict told her he was going to be helping Bernie build the props for the nativity play, so they would no doubt be seeing plenty of each other in the weeks leading up to Christmas. Rosamunde was glad. She smiled to herself. Kizzie would be amused at this turn of events. Perhaps they would finally be friends.

გთ

By the time Rosamunde arrived in London the sky was clearing and a weak sun had begun to emerge. She hopped in a taxi to Notting Hill and, before ringing the bell of the terrace's smart red door, took a deep breath. She loved her sister but she knew she would need the extra oxygen. She was right. Within moments she was being squeezed into a tight hug by Rachel who was simultaneously shouting at her children and typing an email on her BlackBerry.

'Sorry, sorry, sorry,' she apologised as she discarded the phone on the tiled flooring of the hallway (*Would it still work?* wondered Rosamunde), pushed back her red curls and examined her sister with what Rosamunde knew was a very critical eye.

'Gorgeous!' she declared before slightly reducing the compliment with, 'Or at least you will be once we've been shopping. And you need to eat more. You're too thin. It's ageing past forty.'

Rachel was exactly the same as always. Rosamunde had known she would be able to count on this, as her sister was a constant sort of person, in a constantly surprising and unconventional fashion. She looked just as glamorous as ever, with her curly red hair beautifully cut, her lips glossy and red in her signature style, and wearing an entirely impractical white cashmere sweater with fur cuffs and black skinny jeans tucked into sky-high boots.

Rosamunde was permitted a brief but fun-fuelled hour with her niece and nephew. Lily and Art were roughly six and three (both conceived with the assistance of IVF) and, despite having no recollection of who she was, they accepted her with the enthusiasm and gregariousness of their mother. Lily was particularly delighted, having been allowed the day off school to see her aunt. They excitedly gave her a tour of the house, chattering over one another and fighting over whose turn it was to hold Rosamunde's hand. The house, an Edwardian terrace, had the same sort of décor she recalled from her sister's old bachelorette pad in Adam Street but on a grander scale. There were zebra print sofas in the sitting room, facing each other on either side of the marble fireplace, and one of the walls was painted a vivid red. It was a style very different from Rosamunde's own – she preferred vintage pieces, from Victoriana to 1950s kitchenware – but it was marvellously dramatic.

By midday Rosamunde was hauled away by Rachel who, after dispatching instructions to the nanny, led her sister off for the important business of shopping and lunch at Harvey Nichols. It wasn't a lifestyle Rosamunde herself would have the energy or the desire to maintain, but it was just the ticket on occasion. A tonic. Just like Rachel.

The shopping was a great success. Rosamunde was persuaded to buy a beautiful midnight blue cocktail dress, strapless with an intricate lace overlay (although quite when she'd wear it she had no idea) and a cream faux-fur coat to replace her tatty old velvet one. A brief stop at the cosmetics counter ensured she was stocked up with various creams and make-up essentials Rachel swore Rosamunde couldn't live without. She loved how contagious her sister's glamour was.

Then, over a late lunch, the sisters barely drew breath as they caught up with each other's news. Her cheeks pink from the champagne bubbles, Rosamunde asked after her sister's love life, a topic that was never dull.

'Oh gosh, well, Simon's delightful as ever,' Rachel replied. Rosamunde eyed her beadily. Simon was Rachel's devoted husband, but she knew full well there would be more to Rachel's love life than Simon.

'And, well, there is the small matter of Andrés. I met him at London Fashion Week – a twenty-three-year-old model with cheek-bones to die for. You'll love him. Can't understand his accent at all – he's Spanish – but truly, he's divine.' Rosamunde couldn't help but smile. Her sister took an unusual approach to marriage but somehow it was impossible to reproach her for her behaviour.

By pudding they had moved on to the topic of Christmas. It was decided Rachel and her family would arrive at Potter's Cove on the 20th December – the day of the local Christmas market – when she and Simon would have finished work (Rachel was an image consultant and Simon a high-flying lawyer), so they could enjoy their first family Christmas in years. There was no question the get-together must take place in Potter's Cove, since it was Bernie's busiest time of year. Rosamunde told her sister about the nativity play, and the story of Joseph and Mary had Rachel spluttering champagne with mirth, at which point she had one of her impulsive ideas.

'Of course!' she shouted, raising glances from their fellow diners. 'A party! We must have a party after the nativity play. It'll be so much fun! We can invite everyone we know,' she declared. 'We'll hang fairy lights all around the house and serve mulled wine and warmed mince pies.'

While recognising that much of the organisation would land on her shoulders, Rosamunde began to feel a flicker of excitement. It had been many years since their last Christmas party and perhaps it was time – finally – to slay the ghost.

10.
AUGUST 1986

The end of the summer holidays had never been so depressing. Rosamunde and Stephen had spent the entire six weeks with one another, which was nothing unusual for summer holidays in Potter's Cove, but this year their budding romance had imbued their time together with such excitement and anticipation that Rosamunde had never felt so alive. She found herself full of boundless energy and with a patience for others she'd never before experienced. When Rachel hogged the bathroom for hours on end she refrained from hammering on the door in frustration. When Clara and Benedict followed Rosamunde and Stephen around the village like a couple of puppies, she hardly minded. Even Granny Dupont's regimental bossiness had failed to irritate Rosamunde this summer.

But when the last day of August dawned and Stephen's father arrived in his Mercedes to collect him Rosamunde found herself clinging to Stephen for dear life, her arms gripped around his slim torso. She was beside herself with anxiety. How could they possibly manage to be apart for a whole year? Would he find another girlfriend as soon as he returned to Reading? Was this just a holiday romance for him? No, she knew that wasn't the case. But she didn't know whether they could keep their feelings alive through letters and telephone calls until next July.

'I'm going to have to go, babe,' Stephen mumbled into her ear as he stroked her hair. Tears sprang to Rosamunde's eyes. She'd been determined not to cry but was suddenly in danger of losing all self-control.

'Hey, don't cry.' Stephen looked at her, rubbing her tears away with his thumbs. 'Look, I'll speak to my parents. Maybe I could come down to Potter's Cove during the Christmas holidays this year?'

'Really?' Rosamunde was suddenly more hopeful. 'Do you think they'll agree?' Stephen smiled.

'I'll work on them. Give me a couple of weeks. I'll call to let you know. And we'll write, okay? I'm rubbish at letters, though, so don't laugh at my spelling.'

'I won't, I promise.' Rosamunde sniffed, under control again, clinging to the hope that Stephen's plan would materialise.

As she stood in the road, waving at the car long after it had disappeared from sight, she determined to make herself a countdown calendar for the days until the Christmas holidays. She would hide away in her bedroom to do this as she recorded the Top 40 on her new tape recorder. Her heart was aching but she would be okay. As long as Stephen loved her she felt she would be all right.

Two weeks later a phone call came, as promised. Rosamunde's heart pounded as Stephen told her his parents had agreed he could visit Potter's Cove for Christmas, but that he wouldn't be able to stay with his grandmother as she'd decided to move to Reading to buy a bungalow near to Stephen's family home. Rosamunde was mortified that Stephen's link to Potter's Cove – and her – was about to disappear.

'It's not a problem,' Stephen told her. She could imagine him shrugging, sitting in the hallway of his house with his back against the radiator, next to the telephone table. She'd never been there but he'd described his house in detail so she could imagine him better.

'But how can you come to Potter's Cove if your gran's not here?' Rosamunde asked, hoping she wasn't being terribly dim.

'Stay with you, of course,' Stephen suggested. 'Why not?'

'But . . . Well, I mean . . .' Rosamunde found herself lost for words. Would her father agree? Of course he would. But Granny Dupont?

'I love the idea!' Rosamunde declared, finally. 'But I'll have to work on my grandmother. I'll call you in a week.'

Granny Dupont wouldn't countenance the idea. She had experienced a very strict upbringing herself and, since her daughter Marguerite's death, had taken on a great part of the responsibility for ensuring Rosamunde and her sister were firmly disciplined. Her job was not especially easy due to the fact that, whenever she went home to Exeter, Bernie was both unable and disinclined to maintain the rigid structure she imposed on the girls. Their childhood had therefore been a strange mixture of complete and utter freedom interspersed with discipline and rigour. Rosamunde knew which she preferred. Unfortunately, since Granny Dupont had retired last year from the girls' school where she taught French, she had started to visit them far more often, which meant her strict regime was being inflicted on Rosamunde at the very age she was ready to rebel. Rosamunde had generally been a biddable child, far more so than Rachel – who at eighteen was now beyond Granny Dupont's reach – but at fifteen she was all set for mutiny. She would not give up on her opportunity to have Stephen to stay at the Vicarage this Christmas. Whatever it took.

Rosamunde tried everything. Pleading. Sulking. Screaming. She decided to ignore her grandmother entirely, remaining mute whenever she was addressed. Nothing worked. Indeed, with every new attempt to get her own way, Granny Dupont seemed to steel her determination further. They were a fearful match for one another, neither prepared to concede defeat. The atmosphere at the Vicarage became so hostile Rachel packed a large bag and decamped to Tim's house indefinitely, and Bernie found himself spending longer and longer in The Dragon's Head each evening.

⁓

'Another pint, Vicar?' asked Shirley, the barmaid. It was a Thursday evening and Bernie was having a breather from the on-going feud at the Vicarage. He looked at his watch. Seven o'clock. The night was young, really. Supper wasn't until eight.

'Please,' he replied and Shirley flexed her arm muscles as she poured another pint of Stiff Sheep Ale.

'On the house, my love,' she said, pushing the pint towards him. 'Still can't get over what a wonderful christening you did for my little Kevin.'

'You're very welcome,' said Bernie with a smile. 'And I don't mind how long you want to keep plying me with free drinks,' he told her. She giggled at this and looked coyly away. She'd always had a soft spot for Bernie, with his sparkly eyes and his beautiful red hair. He wasn't like your average vicar at all. Much more personable. Even her other half, Jim, said as much and he wasn't so keen on the Church.

Bernie settled back on the bar stool and tucked into a bag of pork scratchings. Every so often another friend or parishioner entered the bar and he received a clap on the back and another drink. He was perched at the end of the bar nearest the fire and felt warm and toasty. He was finally thinking he must make a move in order to be back in time for supper when his closest friend, farmer Buster Marden, arrived.

'Bernie,' he nodded. He was the most undemonstrative of men but solid as a rock and loyal as a Labrador. 'Another pint?' he asked, nodding again towards Bernie's glass. Bernie couldn't leave now; Buster would be offended.

'I'd love one,' he said. 'But I shall drown if I drink another pint of ale. Could you get me a whisky on the rocks instead?' he asked. Buster placed the order and soon the men were chatting about local matters, with no embarrassment when pauses fell in their conversation. At such a moment they would look around the pub, surveying the other punters until someone might be remarked upon. By now Bernie was beginning to feel a little hazy and was thinking he really should take his leave when a gaggle of young men wearing drainpipe jeans tripped into the pub. Bernie recognised one of them as Dom Shelton. Bernie had buried his grandmother, Ethel, a couple of weeks ago.

'Reverend!' Dom shouted. 'You must let me get you a drink.' And so it continued until ten o'clock when Bernie found himself unable to speak. A moment later he fell loudly and heavily off his bar stool.

Granny Dupont, who had been summoned by Shirley, was furious. She marched into the pub and, with Rosamunde's assistance, managed to drag Bernie home where he was deposited on the sofa and force-fed black coffee until he was sober enough to talk. At which point he told Granny Dupont in no uncertain terms that he'd had enough of the standoff between her and Rosamunde and that he would decide who could and couldn't be invited to stay at his house. It was the only time Rosamunde had witnessed Bernie raise his voice to Granny Dupont; indeed, the only time she had seen him put his foot down with her.

Stephen Jameson arrived at the Vicarage on the 22nd December carrying a rucksack and a large red poinsettia.

11.

MONDAY 1ST DECEMBER 2014

Richard Thacker's funeral took place just over a week after his death. It was a typical funeral in that it was both deeply sad and surprisingly uplifting. Tears poured from most of the family, friends and acquaintances in attendance during the service, especially during *The Day Thou Gavest*, but the volume of attendees was wonderfully heartening and later, at the wake, there was laughter as memories of Richard were bandied about and most of the guests were quickly drunk on sherry and relief. Rosamunde had only met Richard once but had been immediately charmed by him and she'd decided to attend to give moral support to Bernie.

She had asked her father once which services he preferred to conduct – weddings, christenings or funerals – and she'd been astonished when he'd told her he achieved the most job satisfaction from the last. When quizzed he'd explained that, although it was the one service the client knew nothing about, it was the most important of their life and an honour for him to have conduct of that final farewell. Today she thought she could understand that. Richard had been taken from the world far too early in life but Bernie had seen to it that his funeral was dignified and yet, like Richard, humorous.

He'd made sure his wife and friends had the opportunity to begin their journey through grief and make it to the other side.

∞

The next day Rosamunde was looking for a bit of light relief and decided to stroll down to the church hall to see how Benedict's prop building was getting on. She entered the hall, her nose pink with cold, and was amazed by the quality of the craftsmanship.

'I'm impressed,' she announced.

Benedict looked up from the wooden cradle he was polishing proudly, having created the piece from scratch. He grinned.

'Why, thank you! But you sound a little surprised. I'm offended.'

Rosamunde blushed and apologised. 'It's just that for someone so clumsy you're actually rather talented.'

Benedict stood up. 'You're making it worse,' he teased her. 'Come on, you, let's grab a coffee from The Kiln and try to warm ourselves up a bit. Bloody freezing in here.'

The Kiln was remarkably busy but they managed to find themselves a small table by the window, looking out on to Outer Cove. The tide was high and the sea raged, waves threatening to leap over the wall at any moment. Rosamunde blew at her coffee before taking a comforting sip. Benedict chuckled.

'What?' Rosamunde hadn't quite got used to the fact that they'd embarked on a friendship of sorts since their meeting on the train the previous week. It was so unexpected. Benedict reached out and wiped some cappuccino froth from Rosamunde's top lip. The wonderful thing about Benedict being gay was that he could touch her in what might otherwise be considered a flirtatious manner and there was no question of the action being anything other than platonic.

'So is the set almost finished?' Rosamunde asked.

'Nearly. A few finishing touches and then we're good to start rehearsals. Has Bernie finished the auditions?'

'Yes, apart from the angels, although there's an issue over Baby Jesus. Kizzie is determined Emma should play the part, but she's quite obviously not newborn, and Sarah Little is equally adamant her new baby Henry should be Jesus. Henry's the obvious choice . . .'

'Well, yes, he's a boy, for a start,' Benedict remarked, raising one dark eyebrow.

'But Dad's in turmoil. He doesn't want to upset Kizzie. He thinks she still hasn't forgiven him for the Lady Di Lookalike Competition all those years ago.'

'Ah yes. Well, she should have won. Aside from her hair colour, she was a dead ringer. The hairstyle, the round eyes, the coy look . . .'

'I know. Of course she should have won, but Dad thought it would look like favouritism to let my best friend win. Anyway, it's ridiculous. Of course she doesn't hold that against him.'

'She does.'

'She doesn't!'

'Does.'

'I cannot believe we're having this conversation. Benedict, you are so bloody annoying.'

'I've always wound you up, haven't I? Always known what buttons to press.'

Rosamunde's cheeks were pink with irritation. It was amazing how they could get on so well one minute and revert to a pair of bickering children the next.

'I'm sorry.' Benedict stroked Rosamunde's hand. 'I've just never been able to resist. It's so easy. Like taking candy from a baby. Look, I'd better get back to finish off the set. Will you meet me in the pub tonight? Kizzie and Gerard are coming. I'll buy you supper and I promise not to annoy you.'

'Are you sure you'll manage?' Rosamunde smiled, irritation subsiding.

'Scout's honour,' he promised. 'And you remember how saucy I looked as a Scout,' he added. As Benedict headed off, Rosamunde's eyes were drawn to his pert behind as she tried to recall what he'd looked like in a Scout's uniform.

༄

'You weren't even in the Scouts!' Rosamunde admonished later when they met at The Dragon's Head.

'I know! They wouldn't have me. Must have been after I was thrown out of the Cubs for pushing David Swann in the stinging nettles.'

'It was!' Rosamunde agreed, remembering. 'You beast!'

'He was calling me gay!'

'Well, he certainly knew earlier than the rest of us did.'

Benedict gave Rosamunde a long look and ordered their drinks. 'Keep an eye out for a table while I get these.'

Rosamunde searched around. The pub was busy tonight. It was the weekly quiz evening. Kizzie and her husband would be turning up soon and the four would have supper together before forming a quiz team. Kizzie was thrilled that Rosamunde and Benedict had embarked on a tentative new friendship. Rosamunde wondered now if she had perhaps been a little harsh in her opinion of Benedict. Or maybe it was just that he'd changed. Either way, it was a positive thing all round that they could enjoy a civilised evening at The Dragon's Head together.

Spotting a table near the fire, Rosamunde dashed over and claimed it, dragging an extra stool from another table. Benedict joined her with the drinks (he'd managed to spill his pint on his jeans but a leopard couldn't be expected to change its spots entirely) and soon Kizzie and Gerard arrived. The girls immediately began gabbling while Benedict did his best to get a few words out of Gerard. Then Bernie and Mrs Garfield turned up unexpectedly and dragged stools up to their table to join in with a hearty pub supper and boost their team for the quiz. Tonight's theme was the 1980s, which had them all laughing merrily as they remembered pop stars and films of the era. Even a question about the Zeebrugge disaster couldn't quell the cheery atmosphere of the evening.

By the end of the night Kizzie had graciously agreed that Emma was perhaps not the best choice for Baby Jesus and Mrs Garfield had diplomatically suggested she could be Henry's understudy in case he was struck down by a bout of colic.

As Rosamunde and Bernie staggered up the hill towards home, she squeezed her father's hand. It had been the sort of evening Rosamunde had longed for when she'd been travelling around the world. Like an old, worn pair of slippers, there was nowhere as comforting as home. They approached the back door and were greeted by Gladys, who was feeling put out that she'd had to spend the evening on her own. They hadn't even lit a fire for her. Rosamunde helped herself to a mug of warm milk and headed up to bed with Gladys under her arm. The cat purred appreciatively at the thought of snuggling up with Rosamunde. It would make up for her lonely evening.

'Night, Dad,' Rosamunde called.

That night she dreamt of a grown-up Benedict, dressed as a Scout, playing the part of Baby Jesus in the nativity play. She woke up giggling.

12.
DECEMBER 1986

Rachel had decided they would have a party on Christmas Eve. This was perfect timing as Granny Dupont had decided to spend Christmas with a cousin in Cornwall and was leaving on Christmas Eve morning. Bernie, meanwhile, would be busy working and had agreed to spend the evening until Midnight Mass having dinner at Mr and Mrs Garfield's. He wouldn't be home until long past midnight and the girls had promised everyone would be gone by then. The excitement in the Vicarage on Christmas Eve afternoon was palpable.

Rosamunde and Stephen had spent the morning entwined on the sofa watching a video of *Ferris Bueller's Day Off*, which Stephen had given Rosamunde for her sixteenth birthday and which had them in stitches. Stephen was a complete film buff and planned to be a film director. Rosamunde absolutely knew he would be. Stephen wasn't the sort of person to give up on his dreams.

Now they were charged with the task of decoration while Rachel mixed a creative punch concoction in the kitchen.

'Mistletoe!' Stephen announced suddenly. 'We need mistletoe!'

'Of course! I can't believe we haven't got any! Let's run down to the greengrocers and see if Mr Petherick has any left.'

As they wandered down to the shops Rosamunde thought life really couldn't be any more perfect, when suddenly she felt a tickle on her nose.

'Oh my goodness! Stephen, look! It's snowing! It never snows here! Look!' Rosamunde danced around, grabbing at the flakes as they began to descend thickly. Stephen watched, laughing at her childish glee, then joining in as they pranced down to the village, their hair soon covered with flecks of snow, their cheeks pink with exertion. Every child in the village seemed to emerge from the warmth of their houses to the exciting chill of the snow shower outside.

Later, with the house duly decorated and the sky dark and full of snow clouds, the three took it in turns to bathe and change. Rosamunde was wearing a pink and white polka dot skirt with a lacy black top and her hair was backcombed, framing her angular face and large amber eyes, which she'd lined with black kohl.

A little while before the party was due to start she went into the spare room – currently Stephen's – where she found him rifling through LPs. He was going to be the DJ for part of the evening and then Gerard would take over for the second half of the night. As Rosamunde knocked on the open door he looked up.

'Wow, you look amazing!' Stephen told her and their eyes locked. He dropped the LPs and immediately they began to kiss. And, as they did, Rosamunde could feel a new intensity envelop them. A fierceness that was raw and fuelled with passion. All thought of the party was forgotten as they began to shed their clothes, kissing urgently. After being restrained with each other for so long they were overcome with a sense of abandonment, exploring each other inexpertly but fully for the first time.

As they lay in bed afterwards, it felt as though they were cocooned in their own world. Rosamunde had never felt so adult or complete. She wondered if life would ever be ordinary again. Then they heard the doorbell, followed by Rachel shouting.

'Rosamunde! Where the hell are you? Can you get the door? I'm still doing my make-up!'

They hurried back into their clothes and rushed down to open the door to the first of the revellers. Rosamunde's make-up might have rubbed off entirely but she was glowing so much she thought her recent actions were embarrassingly obvious. But no one seemed to notice and soon the party was in full swing. While Stephen was in charge of the music, Rosamunde acted as the perfect hostess, taking their guests' coats and handing out the punch. Kizzie and Gerard arrived with Benedict, who – predictably – was the first person to spill a drink on the carpet.

Unfortunately, Clara Johnson had wangled an invitation, but she and Benedict were now going out with each other and spent most of the evening smooching under the mistletoe so they weren't too much trouble. In fact, nothing could ruin the evening for Rosamunde and she was itching to tell Kizzie what had happened.

'Kizzie, come with me to the loo quickly,' she said and obediently her friend followed her into the downstairs lavatory.

'What is it?' she asked, searching Rosamunde's face as though looking for clues. And then she smiled. 'You haven't, have you?' she asked. Rosamunde nodded, her eyes bright and glowing.

'Yep, we did it earlier on – just before the party!'

'How was it?' Kizzie asked eagerly. She and Gerard hadn't gone that far yet and she was desperate for details. The two girls stayed whispering in the loo until someone started hammering on the door.

'Come on,' said Rosamunde. 'Let's go and dance. I can hear *Like a Virgin!*' she said.

'How appropriate!' giggled Kizzie, and the pair jiggled through the throng of teenagers to the makeshift dance floor where they strutted their stuff with the abandonment of the youngsters they were.

Then, when Gerard took over the music, it meant Rosamunde and Stephen could spend the rest of the night dancing with each other, one tune after another. They pranced about to The Bangles and Wham! and then cosied up to each other with *Holding Back the Years* and Rosamunde's favourite, *Take My Breath Away.*

Everyone lost track of time and so poor Bernie arrived home exhausted after a busy evening to find far too many drunk teenagers dancing, canoodling and – in one case – throwing up in his house. He remained unruffled, however, instructing Rachel and Tim to dispatch everyone into the snowy village and agreeing they could clean the house in the morning. He thanked the Lord Granny Dupont wasn't around.

By one o'clock on Christmas morning Rosamunde was in bed, her head a little fuzzy. She was about to drop off when she felt Stephen climb in beside her and wrap his arms around her. He was the best Christmas present she could ever have hoped for.

13.

THURSDAY 4TH DECEMBER 2014

I think Gerard's having an affair.'

The prospect was so absurd Rosamunde nearly choked on her gin and tonic. She raised her eyebrows at her friend.

'Kizzie, there are men who have affairs and there are men who wouldn't even dream of it. Gerard definitely fits into the latter category. He's always been so steady and loving. What on earth's going on?'

'Oh, I don't know.' Kizzie slumped on her bar stool and tucked into the open bag of crisps on the bar in front of them. She stole a furtive glance behind the bar to make sure Benedict couldn't hear them. He was at the other end polishing glasses.

'It's just that he's being all weird and secretive. We've been together for so long and, you know, we're generally happy, but since we had Emma I've been so absorbed with her. I suppose I haven't had much time for him. I think he might have looked elsewhere,' she said gloomily.

Rosamunde considered this. Gerard was a quiet soul to begin with, so she'd have found it hard to notice that he was being odd and secretive, but she'd learnt over the years that you could never really know what went on in another person's relationship, even a close friend's.

'I'm sure it's nothing,' she reassured Kizzie. 'Maybe he's just distracted about the job situation.' Gerard's work as a fisherman hadn't been lucrative lately.

'Maybe,' Kizzie agreed but Rosamunde could see she was still anxious. Perhaps the best thing would be to distract her friend from her worries.

'Listen, do you want a diversion from all this? Will you help me organise the party? Rachel's on at me about it and I've done nothing other than send out invitations. I could really use a hand.'

Kizzie brightened immediately and took a notepad and fountain pen from her handbag. There was nothing she liked better than making lists with her beautifully neat handwriting. It was the teacher in her.

By the end of the evening – with the odd helpful suggestion from Benedict (and some less than helpful: Rosamunde thought any waitresses they might employ were unlikely to be persuaded to dress as Christmas elves) – Rosamunde and Kizzie had settled on some provisional ideas about the food and drink and decided on both the decorations they would need and the music (the obligatory Christmas carols and the usual cheesy Christmas songs). The three were feeling very festive by closing time and Benedict agreed to help Rosamunde collect the alcohol from Oddbins in Thatchley the next afternoon.

∽

Thatchley the following day was alive with the anticipation of Christmas, which unfortunately meant there were very few parking spaces. Benedict drove round and round the small town in his old Land Rover, had a near collision with a van as he fought with another car for the van's space (and lost) and finally – with nerves frayed – found a space almost a mile out of town.

It wasn't the most auspicious of starts and Rosamunde wondered how on earth they would manage to haul the alcohol back to the car. They argued about this for some time until agreeing that they would walk to Oddbins together, deal with payment and any other shopping and then Benedict would fetch the Land Rover and drive it round to the shop so that they could load up.

In fact the walk into town was quite beautiful. The weak winter sun bathed everything in a veil of opaque light, the air was crisp and every building seemed to sparkle and gleam. As they approached the shops they found the bustle of busy shoppers contagious and soon they were drawn into every little store along the street, Benedict seemingly as keen as Rosamunde on searching the treasure troves for Christmas gifts.

Rosamunde hadn't intended to do any Christmas shopping – she'd thought she would leave it until the week before as per her tradition – but she found herself spotting perfect gifts for Rachel, Mrs Garfield and Bernie. For Rachel she found a beautiful grey cashmere wrap, for Mrs Garfield some exotic-smelling bath oil and for her father she pushed the boat out and bought a collector's book on butterflies from the antique bookstore and an expensive bottle of Rémy Martin XO brandy – his favourite. Benedict, meanwhile, bought a beautiful necklace for Kizzie and an antique perfume bottle for their mother (he had good taste, Rosamunde had to give him that).

With these purchases under their arms they were about to make their way to Oddbins when their noses were distracted by the mouth-watering scent of fish and chips.

'Are you hungry?' Benedict asked. Rosamunde agreed she was and they decided to delay the real business of the day a little longer.

They took their bundles of hot, tightly wrapped food to a bench in the nearby churchyard. If in doubt Rosamunde always chose to sit in graveyards, rather than in parks or busy shopping streets. She loved their peace and timelessness.

As they sat companionably side by side, tucking into their chips, Rosamunde noticed that the grave opposite belonged to a lady who had died in 1901 and whose name was Clara.

'Do you ever see Clara now?' she asked. Benedict looked up, surprised.

'Never. No, no, no. She would quite possibly murder me if she ever saw me again.'

'Was the end of the relationship so bad?'

Benedict looked grave. He put his chips to one side, his appetite apparently lost.

'You know, Clara pursued me from when we were just kids and in all truth I don't think I ever loved her. I just gave in. You know we split up when we went off to different colleges at eighteen?' Rosamunde nodded. 'Well, I'd never in my life felt such a sense of freedom and relief. I moved on so quickly I almost frightened myself. But Clara didn't. A few years later, in our early twenties, she decided I was "The One" and I didn't stand a chance, especially after I had that car crash. She looked after me so well and I was grateful. I suppose that makes me very weak. I certainly didn't do her any favours by caving in. I wasted years and years of both our lives. But I sort of thought it would all be fine. That we'd get married and have children and be like everyone else.' Benedict paused and sighed.

'Well, then things got very tricky. By our early thirties – when Clara held her breath every time I knelt down to tie up my shoelaces – I realised it was never going to work. I would never love her enough to marry her. So I ended it. I left with a small rucksack and moved back to Mum and Dad's. The night I left Clara took an overdose.'

Rosamunde found herself gasping in disbelief. She'd never heard this part of the story. Why hadn't Kizzie told her?

'I never told anyone,' Benedict said, as if reading her mind. 'Clara survived and swore me to secrecy. I moved back in. I just couldn't handle the guilt. I proposed a couple of weeks later and things improved for a while. But as the years went by and I kept finding reasons to put off our wedding day, I realised I couldn't keep up the pretence. Anyway, you know how things ended eventually, three years ago. Clara had just turned thirty-eight. It wasn't a pretty ending, but at least she knew it had to be final this time. She moved on, at last. She's married with a baby. Now it's me that seems stuck and unable to get on with my life.'

For a brief moment Rosamunde could feel Benedict's pain, like a living being, sitting between them on the bench. Then, as if someone had snapped their fingers, he sat up straight and smiled.

'So that's my sorry life story, Rosamunde Pemberton. Now let's get that booze before the shop closes and our trip will have been for nothing.'

Rosamunde allowed herself to be pulled up off the bench and, with arms linked, they made their way up the high street. As she watched the normal, happy-looking families all around them, Rosamunde felt an enormous sense of comfort in knowing Benedict was her fellow soldier – life had not followed the paths either of them had imagined it would, but there was a solidarity in their past battles and future hopes. They had each found someone who understood them and, despite the odd clash of character, Rosamunde knew this new friendship was one to hang on to.

14.
FEBRUARY 1987

'Say cheese!' shouted Stephen, and Rosamunde turned around and grinned at him, the sea air on deck making her hair fly up on end. Stephen put his camera back in his pocket and joined Rosamunde, putting an arm around her as they watched the looming island of Jersey become larger as the ferry made its steady progress.

'Nearly there!' he remarked, his eyes alive with the anticipation of their romantic trip away.

Rosamunde had been staggered when Stephen suggested they take a ferry to Jersey for a few days during half term. He'd saved up his Christmas money and had enough to purchase two ferry tickets and three nights in a bed and breakfast, with some spare for spending. Rosamunde was touched he wanted to spend his money on a trip away together instead of on a new stereo or something equally likely to appeal to a sixteen-year-old boy. Thankfully when Stephen had suggested the trip a month ago Granny Dupont hadn't been staying, and therefore didn't need to be consulted, and Bernie had agreed even though he must have realised this would mean the pair sharing a room. For the last month Rosamunde had been in a state of excited anticipation and now, finally, the day for the crossing had arrived.

'Look at that beach!' exclaimed Rosamunde as they neared the harbour. The island might have been only a few hours away by ferry from the mainland but the beaches were like something from a tropical hideaway – white sand spreading for miles and palm trees emerging proudly from behind the sea walls.

On disembarking the ferry they made their way to the Weighbridge bus station, lugging their bags along behind them, where they found the right bus for St Aubin, the harbour village where their bed and breakfast was located. Even though it was only February the winter sunshine was generously exuding some warmth and Rosamunde soon felt too hot in her winter jacket, so she took it off and tied it round her waist.

After a short journey they arrived in St Aubin's village and it took them no time at all to track down their accommodation, which was just above an Italian restaurant on the bulwarks. They checked in, feeling terribly grown up, and were shown their room, which was very old-fashioned but clean and perfectly adequate. Rosamunde tested the bed. It was a bit lumpy but it would do. There was an en-suite that had only a shower – no bath – and was tiny, but it was better than having to share a bathroom with other guests. Then Stephen opened the windows and a blast of cool sea air wafted into the room. Rosamunde joined him and they looked out at the nautical scene outside. The tide was high and the boats directly opposite them in the harbour bobbed merrily around, making clinking bell-like noises as the lanyards on the sailing vessels hit the masts in the wind. A couple of geese teased each other on the slipway, as if daring each other to get their webbed feet wet.

'Is it okay?' Stephen asked, turning to Rosamunde.

'It's perfect,' she replied. 'I already feel sad at the prospect of leaving.'

'You're daft,' Stephen grinned and he pulled Rosamunde towards him. 'Shall we go and explore?' he added, but before any exploration outdoors was conducted they started with each other. The bed squeaked noisily and made them giggle but they didn't care. They didn't know anyone here. They were free as birds. For the first time in Rosamunde's life she felt like a real adult – yet without any of the weight and responsibility that comes with adulthood. This was utter freedom.

By the time Rosamunde and Stephen were ready to venture out it was almost dark and so they decided to save their adventures for tomorrow and find somewhere to enjoy an early supper instead. They showered and Rosamunde pulled on her best jeans and her thick navy and white Norwegian jumper. She was about to put some make-up on but Stephen stopped her.

'You're so pretty, you don't need it,' he said, so Rosamunde happily put her blusher and mascara away.

They found a pub at the end of the bulwarks and nabbed a table by the fire, where they ordered scampi and chips in a basket and drank lager shandies. They chattered away and it felt as if, for the first time, they were able to speak without interruptions from family or friends.

'Chips or crisps?' asked Stephen, starting up a game as they tucked in.

'Chips, definitely,' replied Rosamunde, scoffing her fries down. 'Cheese or chocolate?' she asked, getting into the swing of the game.

'Cheese,' he replied.

'Yes, you are quite cheesy,' laughed Rosamunde and Stephen threw a chip at her in reply before pulling her into an embrace.

'Why did you choose Jersey?' Rosamunde asked, then, and Stephen's smile disappeared. He drew himself away from her and took a pensive sip from his drink.

'We used to come here on holiday as a family, every summer until my sister died, and then we never came here again. So I guess it kind of holds good memories for me. My parents thought it would be too sad to come back but I knew it would just make me feel closer to Claire and, I know this sounds a bit naff, but I wanted to share the place with you too, like somehow you'll get to know Claire a little bit by being somewhere she loved.' Stephen looked at Rosamunde, sheepish.

'That's not naff at all. It's lovely. What kind of stuff did you do here?'

'Swimming in the sea, mainly, but it was summer so I don't suppose we'll be able to do that on this trip.'

'Rubbish. I, Rosamunde Pemberton, am no longer a wimp and I pledge that tomorrow we will swim, however cold it might be,' she laughed.

'I'll hold you to that, you nutcase,' replied Stephen, pulling her into his arms again.

As she leant back Rosamunde surveyed the other patrons of the pub and realised she'd not even looked around her until then. She saw a couple in their thirties opposite them, giving each other dark, sultry looks. Were they married, she mused, or having a wild affair? Then she wondered what the other people in the pub might speculate about her and Stephen. Would they think they were run-aways? she wondered, her imagination running amok. She would run away with him if she could, she thought. But she wasn't brave enough and she couldn't do it to Bernie anyway. And in any event, they would soon be in the lower sixth and before they knew it their A Levels would be under their belts. Finally they could make a plan that allowed them to be with each other.

When they fell asleep that night Rosamunde prayed the next couple of days would go slowly – she didn't want this time to end.

'I love you,' she whispered, thinking Stephen was asleep.

'I love you too, babe,' he replied, squeezing her even closer to him.

The next day the pair rediscovered their more childish sides. They explored St Aubin and found a tiny deserted beach hidden behind some rocks where, as Rosamunde had promised, they plunged themselves into the freezing sea. Once they'd dried off they took a bus into St Helier where they mooched around the shops, then found a swimming pool at an enormous building called Fort Regent and took it in turns to dive off the highest diving board.

By the end of the day they were exhausted and decided to venture no farther than the Italian restaurant beneath their room. The scents of cooking food alone were enough to make Rosamunde's mouth water – an inviting combination of garlic, frying onions and fresh prawns. The charming Italian waiter assured them all the fish had been caught that morning by local fishermen so they dined on delicious sea bass served with local vegetables. Both were suitably impressed with the food and rounded the meal off with some ice cream.

By the end of their brief trip away Rosamunde was certain she'd met the man she would one day marry. It seemed ridiculous, she realised, to be able to make such a claim at sixteen but she simply couldn't imagine a more perfect relationship ever existing. When they arrived in Weymouth and were required to say their goodbyes Rosamunde found herself longing for the day when they would no longer need to be apart.

'One of these days I'm going to marry you, Rosamunde Pemberton,' Stephen mumbled into her ear as they hugged one last time. Rosamunde wondered for hours afterwards if she'd imagined those words. On the train journey to Thatchley, as she listened to her Walkman, she played his words over and over again in her head. She was sad to have said goodbye until Easter but she was gloriously happy too. Rosamunde Jameson, she tried out in her head, and then laughed to herself. There was no doubt about it – the future looked bright. So very, very bright.

15.

SATURDAY 6TH DECEMBER 2014

ugger!' exclaimed Bernie, as he poured himself a cup of tea from the cheerful red teapot at the centre of the kitchen table. Rosamunde looked up from the pile of Christmas cards she was reading nosily.

'What?' she asked, her mouth half full of croissant.

'You know it's the Tiny Tots' Christmas party today? Well, Richard Thacker was due to play Father Christmas. I've completely forgotten to arrange for someone else to do it,' he explained, rubbing his bushy white eyebrows.

Tiny Tots was a weekly event devised by Marguerite years ago as a way of introducing pre-school children to the Church, with the added benefit of helping local mothers get to know one another. A brief service took place in the church hall, Bernie chatted to the children about a particular story or other from the Bible – in years gone by often using Rosamunde's teddies as props – and the event ended with tea, cakes and gossip for the parents while the children drank orange squash and ran wildly around the hall. The Christmas party involved a short service followed by a surprise visit from Father Christmas and a festive spread of cake and sandwiches eaten at the tiny wooden tables and chairs – as if made for midgets – spread around the hall.

'There must be someone who could fill in at short notice,' mused Rosamunde. 'How about Benedict?'

'Of course! A great idea. He seems at a loose end these days, when he's not working at the pub. Would you mind ringing him?'

And so it was arranged that Benedict would play the part of Father Christmas. Not only that but he even offered to make some buns for the party, which was a great help as Mrs Garfield had under-catered, not realising quite how many children would be attending.

Unable to resist seeing Benedict in his new role, Rosamunde accompanied Bernie down to the hall that afternoon and helped get the tables and chairs set up. Then Mrs Garfield arrived and they busily arranged all the paper plates and cups around the tables. Mrs G had even thought of festive napkins and party poppers.

Benedict arrived soon afterwards with a tin of buns, which he added to Mrs Garfield's fare in the hall kitchen. They were decorated with garish lime green and bright pink icing and Rosamunde supposed the children would be immediately attracted to them, even though they looked remarkably disgusting. The final piece of the jigsaw then arrived in the form of the children's entertainer. This had been Rosamunde's idea – she knew from Kizzie how children's parties had become these days and thought an entertainer would be just the ticket.

'Hi, I'm Petey, the entertainer from Party Pandemonium,' explained the man as he strutted into the hall and shook Rosamunde's hand. He was absolutely gorgeous and gay without a doubt. She noticed the man immediately clock Benedict, who looked away shyly.

'I'd better get my outfit on,' Benedict told the group as he made his way into the side room with the ancient Father Christmas outfit and beard that had been used annually for about the last thirty years.

'Who is *that*?' asked Petey, his round blue eyes nearly popping out of his head.

'He's called Benedict,' grinned Rosamunde. 'I'll introduce you later.'

'Make sure you do,' replied Petey as he parked himself close to the side room, clearly hoping to get a sneaky view of Benedict changing.

Pandemonium was the right word for it, thought Rosamunde, as the children then arrived with garrulous parents and began racing round the room like a pack of hounds let loose at the Boxing Day meet.

'Today is a very special day,' Bernie began shortly, after Mrs Garfield managed to get everyone to quieten down. 'Because it's our Christmas party. Now I expect you all go to lots of birthday parties, but does anyone know whose birthday it is at Christmas?' he asked.

'It's mine!' piped up a little boy with golden curls, holding up his hand.

'You're right,' agreed Bernie, remembering that Daniel Brooke's birthday was on Christmas Day. 'And you share a birthday with a very special person called Jesus and he's the reason we're able to enjoy this Christmas party today!'

Rosamunde sat back in her chair, enjoying the little service that ensued. At the end of the service, just before the tea was to be served, there was the sound of sleigh-bells.

'Now hang on, everyone,' said Bernie. 'Can anyone hear that noise?' All the little heads bobbed up and down. 'I think that could be sleigh-bells,' Bernie remarked and the next thing they knew

Father Christmas, dressed very shabbily and with a beard that was now more yellow than white, entered the hall with a sack over his shoulder.

'Ho ho ho!' came the booming voice behind the beard. The children were frozen with fear and delight.

'Have we all been good children this year?' asked Benedict, as he took a seat at the front of the hall.

'Yes!' promised the children.

'Well, in that case I think you should come and get a small present each from me, just to keep you going until Christmas Day.' The children raced up to him and Benedict was besieged.

'Form an orderly queue now, ducks,' Mrs Garfield told them and soon Benedict's job was done. He escaped to change whilst Rosamunde and Mrs Garfield brought out the food. As predicted, Benedict's buns were a popular choice. As the children devoured their treats, the entertainer began to blow up balloons and twist them into the shapes of various animals and, when the children seemed to lose interest in that, he began some magic tricks. It was halfway through a particularly interesting trick that Daniel Brooke started to look a little green.

'I feel sick,' he said, before throwing up all over his plate.

'Me too,' said his neighbour and soon most of the children were throwing up their hastily consumed tea.

'What on earth have you given them to eat?' asked Mrs Brooke, as she grabbed hold of Daniel.

'I'm so sorry,' apologised Mrs Garfield. 'I've no idea what could have gone wrong.'

'Erm, actually I think it could be my fault,' admitted Benedict as he surveyed the mess around him. 'I made those buns,' he said pointing to one of the garish creations. 'And they hadn't finished cooking by the time I needed to leave so I took them out early to ice them before coming here. They could be a little undercooked.'

Mrs Brooke grabbed one of the buns and ripped it in half. The bun was half sponge and half uncooked goo.

'A couple of the eggs may have been slightly past their best too,' Benedict continued, flinching.

'Utterly irresponsible,' Mrs Brooke declared before marching off with Daniel in tow. The children's entertainer – who Rosamunde had been certain would make a play for Benedict before the day was up – now looked at Benedict as if he was a kiddie poisoner and left without another word.

Soon the poorly children had been taken home and Bernie, Mrs Garfield, Rosamunde and Benedict were left to clear up the remains of food, party poppers and sick. Kizzie would have remained to help but Harriet was one of Benedict's victims and was vomiting all over the place.

'Good job, Benedict,' Rosamunde told him, unable to suppress a smile at the disastrous event. Benedict looked suitably hangdog and no one could be cross with him for long, especially as he'd managed to blow his chances with the children's entertainer.

'Shall we go for a drink?' suggested Bernie, when the hall was finally clean and spruce.

'Best idea I've heard all day,' replied Mrs Garfield and the four of them made their way to The Dragon's Head, giggling now at the horrors of the afternoon.

'I think the drinks had best be on me,' said Benedict sheepishly.

'I'd better keep an eye on you, though,' said Rosamunde teasingly. 'After all, we wouldn't want you to poison us.' Benedict looked at her, hurt, and she gave him a hug. Poor Benedict. Such a disaster. But she must have mellowed over the years as, instead of him driving her mad, all she could feel for Benedict was affection.

16.
MARCH 1987

Rosamunde was chopping carrots in the warmth of the kitchen when her life changed forever. Mrs Garfield was making supper with Rosamunde's help and Rachel was at the kitchen table reading a *Seventeen* magazine. Bernie was fiddling with the radio, trying to find Radio 2. Having tuned it in, he joined Rachel at the table with his diary, with a view to reminding himself of the various events taking place that week.

The kitchen clock hands gradually crept towards eight o'clock, just as the news began to be delivered from the radio. It wasn't on especially loudly but suddenly it was as if the volume had increased, all of its own accord. As Rosamunde stood, frozen, she seemed to hear only every three words: 'Zeebrugge . . . ferry . . . return . . . Dover . . . capsized . . . feared . . . dead.' She began to speak over the newsreader.

'Stephen,' she said. 'Stephen went to Zeebrugge today with his parents. They're on a day trip from Dover. There was an offer in the paper.'

Rosamunde saw a flash of panic wash over her father's face before he spoke calmly, reassuringly.

'I'm sure he'll be fine, darling. There are probably lots of ferries doing that trip today. Even if they are on this one, I'm sure everyone will be fine. The rescue operation has already started.' But Rosamunde knew. She knew from the moment she heard the news broadcast that he was dead. She felt it in every inch of her frozen body.

'Heavens above, she's gone quite blue,' fussed Mrs Garfield as she grabbed Rosamunde's cold hands. 'Let's get you into bed where you'll be warm. I'll bring you up a tray. There's no point trying to call his house tonight. They won't be back until late. You get a good night's sleep and we'll call in the morning. He'll wonder what all the fuss was about.'

Rosamunde allowed herself to be steered upstairs, where Mrs Garfield dressed her in pyjamas and tucked her into bed. Half an hour later she brought up a tray of food, which she collected later in the evening, finding it untouched. Rosamunde sat up against the pillows, her eyes wide open, completely still. She remained in this position until dawn when she got out of bed, crept downstairs and dialled the number she knew by heart. There was no answer.

The hours that followed were the darkest she had known since her mother's death. She was protected from hearing the news reports, but was updated by her father and Mrs Garfield, who made endless enquiries. It appeared Stephen and his parents had indeed travelled on the fated ferry – the MS *Herald of Free Enterprise* – that had capsized moments after leaving the Belgian port of Zeebrugge on its way back to Dover. However, it seemed impossible to find out if they had been rescued. Rosamunde found herself existing in a strange bubble of numbness as frenzied activity took place around her. Her father spent most of the day on the telephone whilst Mrs Garfield made endless cups of tea that sat beside Rosamunde, steaming at first and then cooling until an orange rim formed on the insides of the mugs. She couldn't bring herself to allow anything past her lips.

Anxious glances were passed between her sister, father and Mrs Garfield as it became more and more likely Stephen had not survived. By the next morning Bernie had managed to ascertain from Stephen's grandmother that he and his parents were missing, presumed dead. Rosamunde had known this in her heart, but the confirmation from her father packed like a physical punch. She actually found herself falling to the floor, her limbs caving in under her. Then she heard a noise, a strange wailing sound like nothing she'd heard before. It took several moments before she realised this strangled sound of grief was coming from her own lips.

⌖

Within such a short space of time Rosamunde had found herself hurled from a life in which she happily pottered along in an unexciting yet fulfilling pattern of school, homework, chatting with Stephen, supper and bed, to a world in which a new, unhappy pattern had taken over consisting of tears, anger, numbness and a broken sort of sleep in which she was teased with blissful, momentary dreams of Stephen. She barely ate. She couldn't get out of bed. When she hadn't washed her hair for three weeks she received a visit from Granny Dupont.

As Rosamunde continued to stare vacantly out of her bedroom window Granny Dupont sat on the edge of the bed, her leather driving gloves clasped in her hands.

'I know you think of me as an old battleaxe who knows nothing about life,' she began. 'But I was young once, you know. I was in the Air Transport Auxiliary – the ATA – during the war.' Rosamunde kept her gaze fixed on the trees outside.

'It was terrifically exciting. Women had never before had such opportunities. I was lucky – my father was an absolute aeroplane fanatic and taught me to fly when I was only sixteen. So when I was recruited to join the ATA during the war it was the most thrilling time of my life. Us girls were split into two groups, really – the head girls and the glamour girls. Which do you think I was in?'

Rosamunde looked at her grandmother. She spoke, her voice husky from lack of use. 'The head girls,' she said, almost certain. Granny Dupont laughed.

'Wrong. I was a glamour girl. I must show you some photos. I wasn't bad looking back then and I always wore red lipstick – much like Rachel does now. I remember I used to apply my lipstick after I'd landed, before I emerged from the plane. There were always so many dashing men around. One could never be sure when one was going to meet the man of one's dreams.'

Rosamunde found herself astonished. 'What sort of planes did you fly?' she asked.

'Oh, all sorts. Hurricanes. Mustangs. But Spitfires were my favourites.'

'You flew Spitfires?' Rosamunde was amazed. How did she not know this?

'Oh yes. So much fun to fly. Dangerous, though. Our job was to deliver them from the factories to the RAF bases. The worst thing was the weather. There was no radio system. I had three close friends in the ATA and two of them died when their planes crashed in bad weather.'

'What happened to the other one?'

'Ah, Maggie. She was my very best friend. Her plane caught fire on the runway. I watched her land and was bursting with excitement to tell her about a date I had lined up for that evening. I watched the plane go up in flames.' Granny Dupont looked pensive. 'There was nothing I could do.' She took a breath. 'So you see, I may seem hard and cold to you, my dear, but I know what grief is like. I know what it's like to be young and full of hope and then young and full of despair. Maggie wasn't the last person I loved who died back then, but her death was the one I felt very badly.'

'What did you do?' Rosamunde asked. 'How did you cope?'

'I got in my plane that afternoon and then I went on my date that evening. He turned out to be your grandfather.'

The next day, with clean hair, Rosamunde returned to school. She was battered and bruised emotionally, but she'd found a reserve of strength within. If her grandmother could fly a warplane after witnessing the death of her best friend, then Rosamunde Pemberton could take a maths test.

17.
MONDAY 8TH DECEMBER 2014

It was the sort of gloomy December day that never seems to get light but Rosamunde was happily sitting at the scrubbed kitchen table with a steaming mug of tea writing her Christmas cards when Bernie bustled in from the village with various pieces of news.

'Here,' he said, simultaneously switching on the kettle and yanking off his dog collar. 'Guess who I saw in the newsagent's?' This was a rhetorical question, as they both knew Rosamunde could be there all morning trying to guess the answer.

'I don't know,' she replied. 'Who?'

'Bert Clarkson from Clarkson, Petty & Partners. He asked after you.'

Rosamunde smiled. She'd worked at the firm soon after qualifying in law, having decided to pursue a gentle career in the quiet town of Harbourton, an easy half-hour car journey from Potter's Cove, rather than join her fellow students in their ambitious pursuit of jobs in City law firms.

'How was the old boy?' she asked, remembering fondly how delightfully old-fashioned he had been. Every day at noon his secretary had brought him a glass of sherry and a small bowl of dry-roasted peanuts; meetings were to be conducted strictly in the mornings (and then only after 10 o'clock), and he left on the dot of six every single evening. He was an excellent lawyer – meticulous and thorough – but very much part of a dying breed in the legal profession.

'He was well. A little redder in the face. Purple really. But seemed in good spirits. He said he'd always have a job for you if you were interested.'

Rosamunde put down her fountain pen and thought about it. Could she ever go back? Could she somehow manage to locate that legal brain of hers she hadn't used in fifteen years?

'That's sweet,' she said. 'But when I gave up law all those years ago I never intended to go back to it.'

Bernie frowned and made himself a coffee. She knew he thought she was making a mistake – he'd been so proud of her job as a lawyer – but he knew better than to try to dissuade her.

'Do you know what you will do?' he asked, sitting himself down in the large pine chair at the end of the table.

'I do have an idea, actually,' Rosamunde replied. 'You know I did a lot of work in wildlife sanctuaries when I was away?' Bernie nodded. 'Well, I felt like I'd really found my vocation. So I've arranged an interview at Harbourton Wildlife Park. I know I don't have any official qualifications but I'm hoping my experience will count for something. I did a lot of work with orang-utans in Borneo, so that should help.'

Bernie sighed. He knew all about pursuing a vocation. He'd worked in a bank prior to training as a vicar and although his career decision had made him poor in material wealth, it had enriched his soul no end. He understood.

'They'd be fools not to snap you up,' he declared. 'Now I'm off to see Mrs Croft about her daughter's wedding.' He stood up and pulled on his voluminous coat again. He'd just stepped outside the back door when Rosamunde spotted his dog collar on the kitchen worktop.

'Wait!' she shouted as Bernie reached the end of the path. 'Your dog collar!'

'What would I do without you?' Bernie asked as he took the collar gratefully from Rosamunde and ruffled her hair.

As Rosamunde hurried back into the warmth of the Vicarage she thought about her prospective post. It would be good to have the structure of a proper job again if she was lucky enough to get it. But for the rest of today – while she was free as a bird – she decided she would have one of her 'being days'. She had learnt about these when travelling in the Far East. A fellow traveller she met in Thailand had explained how Western culture was almost exclusively focused on doing whilst Eastern life made time for just being, whether this involved meditation, prayer or simply people-watching by the side of the street. Since this revelation she'd decided to indulge herself with such a day intermittently and found it almost always brought a sense of peace and direction to her life.

She started by lighting the fire in the sitting room. No sooner had she done this than the sun began to break through the murky clouds outside and sunshine started to stream through the French windows. She lay down in a pool of light on the carpet and relished the warmth of the sun on her face and the sound of the whooshing flames in the fireplace. Soon she heard another familiar, comforting sound as a loud purring started up beside her. There was a lot Rosamunde could learn from Gladys, who, as far as she could tell, had nothing but being days.

She didn't think about anything in particular as she lay there. She just focused on her breathing and the scents and sensations around her. She was immersed in a feeling of utter relaxation when she suddenly heard a loud sound outside. Immediately both she and Gladys were alert – eyes open, ears pricked. Then the doorbell rang. So much for her day of peace and quiet.

'I'm so, so sorry, Rosamunde but I seem to have crashed the Land Rover into the garden wall.' It was Benedict. 'I'm sure I can fix it, though,' he added quickly.

'Well, that's okay, then,' Rosamunde replied archly. 'Did you have any particular reason for coming here and destroying the place?'

'No, not really,' Benedict admitted. He clearly wished he had a suitably noble reason that would in some way make the garden wall incident a small blip by comparison. Then his face lit up as if he'd had a brainwave.

'Actually, there was something. I know Bernie's looking for recruits for the choir. I was coming to offer my services.' He seemed proud of his quick thinking but Rosamunde was bent over as if in pain. When she managed to stand up again he saw she was crying. With laughter.

'Oh, I'm sorry, Benedict, but really, you're tone deaf. Remember that Christmas the Cubs were asked to sing at the carol service? It was just before you were thrown out, I think. And you had to sing a verse of *Away in a Manger* all on your own? The whole church was fidgeting as they tried to contain their laughter. It was dreadful.'

Benedict looked hurt.

'Oh for goodness' sake, come in!' she told him, hauling him into the kitchen. She'd think about the wall later.

It transpired that Benedict was at a loose end and hadn't thought about having a being day himself. He didn't have any shifts at the pub and his inspiration for turning pots had yet to re-emerge. Even his set building for the nativity play was done. He made various suggestions about what they could do for the rest of the day but Rosamunde decided instead to introduce him to the philosophy of just being. They lay on a sofa each in the sitting room, chatting and then not chatting, peeling satsumas meticulously and savouring the scent of Christmas just around the corner. Eventually, they decided to get some fresh air so they went for a stroll down to Inner Cove, where they perched on rocks and looked out to sea.

When darkness descended they returned to the Vicarage, where they were obliged to stop being and start doing. Benedict chopped vegetables whilst Rosamunde put a leg of lamb in the Aga and made some mint sauce. Bernie arrived home with hilarious tales about Mrs Croft's obsessive wedding planning and soon Mrs Garfield trotted in with a homemade apple and blackberry crumble to be warmed for their pudding later in the evening. After dinner the four played Rummy and Pontoon by the fire as they listened to Christmas carols, much to Bernie's dismay – he'd heard enough carols for a lifetime.

When Rosamunde headed up to bed with a hot water bottle, having dispatched Benedict and Mrs Garfield into the night, she thought that perhaps the key to proper relaxation was to enjoy the perfect mix of being and doing. She was just drifting into a relaxed slumber when she remembered the garden wall. She sent a text message to Benedict from her phone: 'Tomorrow is a doing day . . . xxx'

18.
APRIL 1987

Only two weeks after Rosamunde had returned to some semblance of normality, though her heart was sore and her body rake-thin with grief, she began to realise there were other changes to her body that had been taking place recently.

A trip to the school nurse confirmed her suspicions. She was possibly the only sixteen-year-old in the history of time to be elated by an unplanned pregnancy. A visit to the doctor a few days later revealed that she was about nine weeks gone. Bernie, while not exactly happy about the situation, was reassuringly supportive following the news and spent most of each day trying to pluck up the nerve to tell Granny Dupont. When he'd finally got round to it he reported that, most surprisingly, Rosamunde's grandmother was uncharacteristically unruffled by the news. She'd even promised to start knitting a matinee jacket.

There was no doubt it was scandalous news in the village, however, particularly as Rosamunde was a vicar's daughter, but whilst everyone around her reeled at the shock of the situation and tried to cajole her into making plans, Rosamunde was lost in a bubble of contentment. She sat in lessons stroking her still flat stomach and wondering whether the baby would inherit Stephen's turquoise eyes and, as her classmates focused on *To Kill a Mockingbird*, Rosamunde found herself going through the alphabet in her head, choosing baby names. Every now and again she'd feel a sharp pang of grief slice through her body as she wished she could be sharing this joy with Stephen, but then she recognised that if he'd still been alive there was every chance both he and she would have been as shocked and horrified at this pregnancy as everyone else. As it was, Rosamunde felt she had been given a gift. A link forevermore with the boy she had loved so desperately.

The only other person who seemed to be as excited about the whole situation as Rosamunde was Kizzie. She was going through a bit of a hippy phase, obsessed with horoscopes and certain that everything that happened in life was down to fate. Rosamunde's pregnancy was, to her, absolute confirmation of this belief.

On one particularly rainy April day the girls sat on the bus home from school and Kizzie chattered about how the baby would have a dramatically different personality depending on which star sign it was. Rosamunde wasn't really into what her father called 'Kizzie's twaddle' but she listened happily, grateful for any positive interest in the baby. As Kizzie twittered on, Rosamunde decided she would make her a godmother. Then she started to think about who else she would choose. She'd definitely ask Mrs Garfield – she, too, had been very supportive since the news had broken. She hadn't been blessed with children and had told Rosamunde she was looking forward to being able to play grandmother. She was a little bit stuck for godfathers but she supposed she could always ask Gerard, Kizzie's boyfriend, at a push. The other boys she knew at school were far too irresponsible for such a job.

As the bus arrived in Potter's Cove, Kizzie was still rabbiting on about the disadvantages of being born a Scorpio when Rosamunde felt a twinge in her pelvis. She frowned.

'Are you okay?' Kizzie noticed immediately. 'What's up?'

'Oh, nothing. It's fine,' replied Rosamunde. She'd had a few twinges in the last few days but her doctor had said it was normal. There were so many changes going on that she was bound to feel a few aches and pains. 'Hey,' she said, changing the conversation. 'Do you fancy going to the cinema later? We could go and see *Lethal Weapon*.'

'Yes!' Kizzie agreed immediately. 'If only to see Mel Gibson. I love that man!'

Rosamunde returned to the Vicarage for a bath and to change into leggings and an off-the-shoulder sweatshirt. Bernie offered to drive the girls to the cinema in Thatchley and it was agreed they would get the bus home. She promised to be back by eleven o'clock.

As fate would have it, however, Rosamunde didn't make it home at all that night. Halfway through the film she went to the lavatory and by eleven she'd been driven to hospital in Totnes by Kizzie's mother. Rosamunde was examined and as she sat there, expectant, a young doctor confirmed her worst suspicions.

'I'm sorry,' he told her. 'You've had what's called a miscarriage.' He took in her sad, youthful face. 'Listen,' he said. 'It's probably for the best. You're far too young to be a mother. You'll get another chance when you're older.' He meant well, Rosamunde was sure, but she couldn't look at him. She turned her head away and shut her eyes.

Strangely, for a day or two after the miscarriage, Rosamunde found herself weirdly elated – as if a weight had been lifted from her. She laughed hysterically at witty remarks her father and Kizzie made and she even made a few jokes herself. But soon a black veil of gloom and despair descended until Rosamunde felt as though she were flying solo encased in murky cloud, much as Granny Dupont and her friends must have felt when they were flying Spitfires in terrible weather during the war.

The next few weeks were a blur that Rosamunde would never fully remember, for which she was grateful. It was the lowest point of her short life, of that she was certain, the loss of the baby compounding the grief for Stephen that had been neatly parcelled away when she'd discovered she was pregnant.

It was about a month after the miscarriage that Rosamunde woke up in the night, breathless. She'd been dreaming that she was being suffocated. She was with Stephen and the long-nosed, sinister child catcher from *Chitty Chitty Bang Bang* had locked them in her bedroom. Rosamunde screamed as he picked up her pillow and began to smother Stephen. She tried to reach out to him, to save him, but her limbs were heavy and soon the child catcher had pinned her down and was trying to suffocate her as well. Rosamunde could feel the pillow being squashed down onto her mouth as she fought for oxygen.

As she sat up in bed, gasping for breath, she wondered whether she would actually have died if she hadn't woken up at that moment. She realised this was fanciful but it made her recognise that she didn't want to lie down and die. She'd lost Stephen and now she'd lost his baby, but she didn't want to lose herself as well.

It was a turning point for Rosamunde. She would possibly never be quite the same girl again but she had to find something to grasp on to. Something to keep her afloat. The raft she decided to cling to was her studies. She had her O Levels coming up and she'd been anything but focused in recent months. If there was one area of her life she could influence it was this.

Rosamunde achieved straight As in her exams and again, two years later, in her A Levels. With determination she had transformed herself from a victim of life's cruel events to a high-flying achiever.

The first chapter of her life was closed.

PART TWO

PART TWO

19.

WEDNESDAY 10TH DECEMBER 2014

Benedict had always been wild about dogs and on a crisp, December day – as an early Christmas present to himself – he was collecting a rescue greyhound from Totnes to replace his old Labrador, Tess, who'd died a year ago. Rosamunde had agreed to go with him for moral support – he was worried he'd come home with every greyhound in the centre if he wasn't physically restrained. It was no hardship to Rosamunde, who loved any contact with animals, whether pets or wildlife. She assured Gladys she wouldn't bring a greyhound back to the Vicarage and strolled down the hill to The Kiln where she'd agreed to meet Benedict for today's adventure. She was rather enjoying their little jaunts. Rosamunde had told Benedict she needed to be back by mid-afternoon, however, as she was helping Bernie pick the angels for the nativity play. She had no qualms about favouritism (unlike Bernie) and had mentally picked Harriet, Kizzie's little girl, already. She would use impartial judgement to help elect the other five. But for now she had several hours to dedicate to Benedict.

Benedict had already had his house assessed by the couple who ran the home and clearly they had the measure of him for, when they arrived to a cacophony of barking, Phil and Suzie told Benedict very firmly they had just the dog in mind for him. Benedict's large dark eyes were full of pity and sadness as he and Rosamunde were led past the many kennels until they reached the greyhound that had been earmarked for him. They opened the kennel door and, instead of bounding up, the dog looked up from his bed, scrutinised Benedict and then rested his head back down with a sigh, as if to say, 'I've nearly been chosen so many times that I can't be bothered to make the effort today. If you like me, then have me, but I'm blowed if I'm going to do all the running.'

The dog was black, skinny and long-limbed, with dark eyes as soulful as Benedict's and a long Womble-like nose. He had a little white diamond patch on his chest, which made him look like Bernie in his cassock and dog collar, and Rosamunde found herself instantly smitten. Benedict approached the dog bed and knelt down beside the hound, stroking his silky coat.

'What's his name?' he asked Suzie, who was looking on fondly.

'Humphrey,' she told him.

'Really?' asked Benedict. 'Well, that seals it, then, old chap,' he told the dog. 'I had a favourite teddy called Humphrey once,' he explained to the onlookers sheepishly. 'I lost him when I was about seven and I never managed to find a bear to replace him. I think I may finally have found his substitute.' Humphrey seemed to agree. He raised himself from his bed and began, very slowly, to wag his tail.

On the way home, with Humphrey happily dozing on the back seat, Rosamunde found herself being quizzed by Benedict about her love life.

'Have you met anyone since you got back to the village?' he asked. Rosamunde raised her eyebrows at him.

'Are you joking? I love Potter's Cove with all my heart but it's hardly throbbing with eligible bachelors. Apart from you, of course,' she added quickly. 'But you don't count.' Benedict pulled a face.

'Anyway, I'm not looking. What about you?' Rosamunde turned the tables. 'Anyone special?'

'Only Humphrey,' he grinned. 'And I think we make a very special couple.' Rosamunde smiled. She was inclined to agree.

ꙮ

Later in the day the Vicarage was taken over by a gaggle of over-excited little girls and their parents. The auditions had been meant to take place in the church hall but the heating had broken down and Bernie didn't feel he could inflict the creepy, cold building on a bunch of small children. It was hardly ideal, though, and the Vicarage seemed to groan like an elderly aunt wakened by an overzealous young relation as she dozed by the fire. Doors were slammed, voices were loud. It was all less than angelic.

Thankfully Mrs Garfield turned up in the nick of time, just as Bernie and Rosamunde were standing in the sitting room, unsure how to get the children and their parents to quieten down suffi-ciently to start the auditions. Kizzie had been unable to stay with Harriet; otherwise she would have done her teacher bit. Within a couple of minutes Mrs Garfield had commanded silence and was ordering everyone about. An hour and a half later the auditions were over and the successful angels had been notified, includ-ing Harriet who, to be honest, was far too loud and bossy for an angel, but Rosamunde had insisted. She'd even been made the Angel Gabriel.

With the house returned to the three of them, they sank into the sofas, breathing a collective sigh of relief. Gladys emerged from the airing cupboard where she'd taken refuge for the last couple of hours and deigned to re-join the rest of the household by the fire.

'I don't know why I think it's a good idea to do these things,' Bernie admitted. 'Such a fabulous wheeze in August but now

I remember why I always feel in such dire need of a break by January,' he grumbled.

'Oh, don't be such a Scrooge,' Mrs Garfield admonished him. 'I think it's lovely to have a nativity play in the village. It gets everyone involved as a community, like the old days. What you need is a stiff drink and a decent meal,' she announced, getting up from her slumped position on the sofa.

'Now that's a wonderful idea,' he agreed, starting to haul himself up.

'No, no,' she told him. 'You stay there. I'll get the food on and Rosamunde will sort out the drinks, won't you, dear?'

'Of course,' Rosamunde agreed. Who could refuse dear Mrs Garfield? She jumped up and began to inspect the drinks tray on the shining chestnut table in the corner of the sitting room. There were numerous bottles containing all sorts of putrid-coloured potions but she located the important bottles – gin for her and Bernie, sweet sherry for Mrs Garfield, who always liked Harvey's Bristol Cream as an aperitif as Christmas approached.

'No Benedict tonight?' asked Bernie as Rosamunde fixed the drinks. He had become rather a part of the furniture of late.

'No, he's settling Humphrey in.' Rosamunde proceeded to tell her father about their morning.

'He's a funny lad,' Bernie mused. 'Has he found himself a partner since all that Clara business?' he asked, the modern word 'partner' sounding foreign on his tongue.

'Maybe he did initially, but there's no one at the moment,' Rosamunde replied, thinking to herself what a waste it was that he was single. Her view of him had changed dramatically in the last couple of weeks; witnessing how soft he was at the greyhound centre today had cemented her new opinion of him. 'It's such a waste,' she added, speaking her mind.

'Well, he's not the only one who's going to waste,' Bernie remarked, one white eyebrow raised, his amber eyes fixed on Rosamunde. But Rosamunde would not rise to that particular bait. Instead, she took a large gulp of gin and tonic and flicked on the television. There was some dreadful-looking dating show on Channel 4. That would do, she decided. Let her father focus on the love lives of this lot. Anyone's rather than her own.

20.
APRIL 1997

It was the spring of 1997 and Rosamunde was still working at Clarkson, Petty & Partners in Harbourton, where she'd bought a small flat overlooking the harbour. She'd worked there since qualifying as a lawyer despite the opportunities she'd had to pursue a career in London after obtaining a first-class honours degree in Law from Durham University.

Having focused on her studies so obsessively, Rosamunde had found little time to open her heart to the men who'd pursued her over the last decade. She'd enjoyed the odd fling but had swiftly severed relationships before there was a chance they might turn serious. At twenty-six, though, she was beginning to watch all her friends pair off. Suddenly, instead of wobbling drunkenly from bar to bar with Rosamunde on a Saturday night, they were making excuses. 'Sorry, Rosamunde. Toby's cooking for me tonight. A romantic candlelit dinner,' or 'Would love to but I'm meeting the in-laws this evening.' It was all rather disappointing and made Rosamunde start to question her own love life, or rather the lack of it. So at last she opened her eyes a little. Of course, now that she was looking it seemed there was a terrible drought of decent men.

Beginning to think she was never going to meet anyone, Rosamunde threw herself into her work. She was dealing mainly with personal injury claims at the moment, which was hardly terribly challenging but she liked helping ordinary people rather than making rich conglomerates even richer. She was in the midst of a case that was pulling at her heartstrings and she had a meeting arranged with the client this morning.

'Good morning, Mr Chapworth,' she said, helping his wife usher him into the meeting room. The room was on the ground floor of the old building and had large sash windows looking onto the street. Although beige blinds prevented passers-by from gawping in at confidential meetings, they still allowed the sunshine to burn through and so the room was bright and warm.

'Would you like a tea or coffee, either of you?' she asked the couple, who were in their fifties but looked much older. They were sitting down now at the round conference table and looked terribly awkward. This was by no means their first meeting with Rosamunde but the Chapworths were simple folk and they were as uncomfortable in a law firm as a farmer in a suit. They shook their heads and so Rosamunde pulled the door shut and sat down beside them. She'd never been the kind of lawyer to sit opposite her clients in an authoritative fashion.

'Thank you for coming in,' she told them. 'I just wanted to update you on my recent meeting with the other side. As you know, the trial date's fixed for next week but negotiations are going well and it's clear Lenses 4 U doesn't want the adverse publicity of a trial so I'm hopeful we'll be able to reach a very decent settlement. I'm adamant we shouldn't go below the figure we discussed, though, and we're about twenty thousand pounds away from that at the moment,' she explained. 'So I wanted to discuss the next step with you,' she added. 'What I need to know is how you feel about the trial. If you desperately want to avoid it we can settle at the sum currently offered but I would recommend holding out for the extra money, although there is a risk that in doing so we'll end up having to go to trial.'

She looked at the couple, who were listening eagerly to her every word, and her heart ached for them. Mr Chapworth had made his living as a children's book illustrator and although he'd never made an enormous amount of money from his work, the stylistic pictures were well recognised and his living was sufficient to get by on. Not enough to enable Mrs Chapworth to give up her job as a dinner lady at the local primary school, and not sufficient to allow either of them to retire early, but they were happy with their lives. Or, at least, they had been until Mr Chapworth's optometrist had failed to diagnose glaucoma despite obvious warning signs. Without an early diagnosis Mr Chapworth's vision had deteriorated swiftly and he was now registered blind.

He would never have thought to sue the opticians but his nephew, who had a good business mind, suggested he should look into it and after some persuading from Mrs Chapworth he had contacted his local law firm – Clarkson, Petty & Partners. And so it was that Rosamunde had been assigned to the case, and she'd developed a very soft spot for the couple. She'd gone far beyond the call of duty and had even made arrangements with the Guide Dogs for the Blind Association. Mr Chapworth was due to become acquainted with his guide dog, Indigo, within the month and Rosamunde sincerely hoped having the dog would give him more confidence to go out. Mrs Chapworth had confided in her recently that the poor man had lost all self-assurance now that he could no longer do his job or see properly and could hardly bear to leave the house.

'I think we should take this to its conclusion,' Mr Chapworth said eventually. 'I don't like the idea of the trial but I want to get the money I deserve now we've come this far.' His voice was soft but determined. He was a gentleman in the truest sense, thought Rosamunde.

There was, however, no need to go to trial in the end. The other side eventually agreed to a sum Rosamunde was prepared to accept on Mr Chapworth's behalf on the eve of the trial date. The settlement figure was generous and showed the firm's desperation to avoid bad publicity, but Rosamunde was applauded by her colleagues too, for her hard work and excellent negotiation skills.

It was a week after the settlement that Rosamunde received a call from the firm's receptionist asking her to come down to collect a bouquet of flowers. Rosamunde skipped down immediately to find a youngish chap standing in reception holding the bouquet.

'Oh, they're beautiful. Thank you,' she said to the man, supposing he was the florist. She took them from him and was about to open the tiny envelope poked into the arrangement to discover who they were from when the man, who hadn't gone yet, spoke up.

'They're from my uncle,' he said. 'He was so grateful for what you did for him.' He looked nervous, his eyes darting about. But as he pushed his glasses up the bridge of his nose Rosamunde found herself intrigued.

'You're the nephew!' she exclaimed. He nodded meekly. 'Oh, I'm so glad you persuaded your uncle to sue. It would have been too awful if he hadn't. He deserved every penny he received.'

'I'm, er, Giles,' he introduced himself hesitantly, shaking her hand. 'I just knew he wouldn't do it unless I stepped in. He's not really the suing type. Thinks it's an American thing to do, but they'd never have managed financially without his income. And it wasn't just that. Those terrible opticians needed to be brought to justice. I'm just sorry there wasn't a trial and that it didn't become public,' he added vehemently. 'I'm sorry – that was an outburst,' he added, looking sheepish.

But Rosamunde was taken with him. He was sweet. And, although he didn't appear to be terribly high-flying, he seemed quite a bit more sophisticated than his aunt and uncle. She saw him shuffle, about to take his leave, and she realised it was now or never. She had never done what she was about to do before.

'I don't suppose,' she said, 'you'd like to go for a drink with me later, would you?' Giles looked up, astonished, as though she might be playing a practical joke on him, and smiled shyly.

∽

That evening she took Giles to the local wine bar for a drink. As they chatted surprisingly easily, Rosamunde tried to analyse what it was about him that – for once – had made her interested in doing the running herself. He was not especially attractive. In fact, he was quite plain, with his pale skin and mousy hair. And there was nothing remarkable about his character. But he had a kind, open face that seemed to reflect his soul. It was as though it was lit up by his goodness, and that was what Rosamunde had decided she needed. She was ready – at last – for a proper relationship and with Giles she thought she might have found what she was looking for. For his part, it seemed he could barely believe his luck.

Giles had also taken a flat in Harbourton but it was sparsely furnished and he had no flair for home decoration, so soon he became a regular visitor to Rosamunde's little apartment. It was the first property Rosamunde had owned and she was very proud of the place despite its shortcomings – mainly a lack of space. There was an open-plan kitchen/dining/sitting room, with cream carpets and French doors leading to a balcony overlooking the estuary, and one bedroom with an en-suite bathroom. She had bought a small round table with a blue and white ceramic top and spindly chairs for the balcony and she had dressed the interior in a country cottage style even though the apartment block was modern and most of the flats were decorated in the minimalist trend that was so popular now. It was a very feminine apartment – full of pretty antiques, ornate mirrors and floral soft furnishings – but Giles was simply glad of the comfort both it, and Rosamunde, offered.

∽

On his first visit to the Vicarage Giles was very nervous.

'I don't know what you're so anxious about,' Rosamunde said as she drove into Potter's Cove and up the hill to her father's house for lunch.

'Well, he's a vicar,' he tried to explain. 'So it's like meeting your prospective father-in-law for the first time and going to confession all at once.'

Giles had been raised a Catholic and seemed to have a rather quaint view of what Bernie would be like. She suspected he'd never met an Anglican vicar before – least of all one like Bernie – and she was too amused to put Giles right. He would discover soon enough that Bernie was a soft, gentle giant. Rosamunde also chose to gloss over Giles's reference to Bernie as his 'prospective father-in-law.' It was true their relationship was moving fast but Rosamunde wasn't ready to start choosing the rings just yet.

As they approached the back door Rosamunde wondered if Giles might actually faint with nerves. He was white bordering on green, and beads of sweat had emerged on his upper lip. Rosamunde wished she could feel a little more sympathy for him, but recently she'd been feeling that Giles had gobbled up the kindness quota in their partnership.

'Rosie!' greeted Bernie as they entered the kitchen. 'I'm just back from morning worship. And you must be Giles,' he said grasping

Giles's sweaty palm. 'It's so wonderful to meet you, old chap. Now, what would you like to drink? Is it too early for a sharpener?'

'A coffee would be great,' replied Giles, looking relieved to discover Bernie was not only human, but a kindly human.

'Really?' Bernie looked a little puzzled, but put the kettle on and proceeded to fix large gin and tonics for himself and Rosamunde. It was actually only half past eleven but Bernie felt a drink was quite essential when it came to social ice-breaking.

'Erm, well, if you're having a drink, then why not?' Giles piped up and Rosamunde nodded at him encouragingly. He may not have been the world's biggest drinker but today was not the day to be abstemious.

Bernie was right, in any event. A little bit of alcohol loosened everyone up nicely and a pleasant Sunday followed. They had drunk too much to be able to drive home and so Rosamunde and Giles decided to stay the night. By ten o'clock Giles had gone up to bed, and Rosamunde and her father sat by the fire with Gladys, the new kitten, who was curled up in Bernie's lap.

'So, what do you think?' Rosamunde asked her father.

'He's lovely. Delightful. He obviously adores you, which is the most important thing.'

'You think he's boring,' she replied.

'Rosie, I'm just so pleased you've found someone, at last, whom you consider serious enough to bring home. Even if he is boring – which I'm sure he isn't – it wouldn't matter so long as he treats you well. But you must love him, my dear. It mustn't be a one-way relationship.'

Rosamunde cocked her head to one side, her red hair cascading onto the sofa arm, deep in thought.

'I do love him,' she told her father. 'In my own way, I do.'

The following weekend wasn't quite as successful. Rachel was down from London for the weekend and Rosamunde feared she might eat Giles for Sunday lunch. It was her turn to feel nervous.

Rachel had her latest man with her – a drummer who'd worked with Oasis and who looked like he'd been up all night. He was devilishly good-looking despite his red eyes and dishevelled locks. Rosamunde found herself immediately embarrassed at Giles's wholesomely fresh face and combed hair and then reprimanded herself. It wasn't as though she wanted a rock star boyfriend, after all.

Bernie tried his hardest all day but it was clear his daughters' men had nothing in common and while Rosamunde felt strained at the effort of trying to make the best of things, Rachel seemed intent on making the day as awkward as possible. She kept mouthing 'D.U.L.L.' to Rosamunde behind Giles's back and when she started to ask him if he'd ever taken drugs Rosamunde decided enough was enough and suggested she and Giles take a walk down to Inner Cove.

'Your sister doesn't like me,' he said sadly as they walked down to the village and across the beach.

'It's not you,' Rosamunde assured him. 'It's just that she's going through a phase. Rachel's been going through phases her whole life and currently it's the ladette phase. Truly, Zoë Ball and Sara Cox have nothing on her. We're not very close at the moment.'

'What a shame,' he said. 'I think she's lovely anyway,' he added. Rosamunde felt her heart sink. Did Giles ever not like anyone? Then she stopped herself. Surely it was a good thing to like everyone? It was, of course, but it was just so difficult to match up to Giles. Being with someone so good made you feel constantly lacking by comparison.

It hadn't been a successful day, but in their everyday life Rosamunde was happy. There were a few issues, but weren't there

113

in any relationship? And he treated her so well. Giles was always surprising her with little gifts or taking her out to dinner.

So when the inevitable day arrived – a year later – and Giles asked for her hand in marriage, Rosamunde found herself, without hesitation, saying yes. She was twenty-seven, a lawyer, and now she was engaged. Rosamunde had finally put her difficult past behind her and was ready to move on.

21.

THURSDAY 11TH DECEMBER 2014

It was two weeks until Christmas and Rachel had just arrived from London in her new sports car, having taken a couple of days off work. She'd left the children with Simon and was clearly in the mood for some fun: she cracked open a bottle of champagne as soon as she arrived through the kitchen door.

'Where's Dad?' she asked.

'He's just cycled into Thatchley for a wedding interview with Mrs Croft's daughter and her fiancé. He should be back soon.'

'Do you remember that wedding interview of yours?' Rachel asked. 'Poor Giles.'

But Rosamunde didn't want to think about Giles. She poured them a glass each and they made their way into the sitting room where she had just lit the fire.

By the time the sisters had finished the bottle Rosamunde had begun to wonder where Bernie had got to. He'd said he would be back by three o'clock and it was nearly five now and dark outside. She was about to phone The Three Bells, the pub where the interview had taken place, when a drenched and out-of-breath Bernie staggered through the back door.

'What on earth's happened?' asked Rachel, stubbing out the cigarette she'd been smoking at the kitchen window while Rosamunde rinsed their glasses. Bernie began to speak but as the story unfolded he found himself crying with laughter. He mopped at his eyes with his dotty hanky.

'What?' Rosamunde laughed. His mirth was contagious. Eventually, Bernie managed to pour the story out.

He'd been cycling home from the pub along the lanes when he'd come across a figure lying prone on the road. Immediately alarmed, he'd hopped off his bicycle to make sure the man was alive. The man – Terry Molton – was the landlord of The Three Bells and a man known for his love of liquor.

'So I woke him up,' explained Bernie, still trying to get a grip of himself. 'And I gave him some water. He was ever so grateful. He'd had a heavy lunch at his sister's house, he told me, and was walking back to the pub. Anyway, he thanked me and picked himself off the ground and when I turned around I saw him cycling off. On my bike!' Bernie guffawed. 'I couldn't believe it! So I had to walk the rest of the way home!'

The three of them were in fits of laughter at this modern twist on the story of The Good Samaritan but finally they recovered and the girls took their father through to the sitting room where he dried off by the fire. Rosamunde made tea and found some cake in a tin, which she brought through, and the three knuckled down to the real business of the day – finalising plans for their Christmas party.

They had now received replies to the invitations and the drink had been collected by Rosamunde and Benedict and was stashed in the garage. Mrs Garfield had offered to do the catering but they wanted her to be able to let her hair down, so they'd asked a caterer from Thatchley to prepare the food instead. It had been decided that the spread should be festive but simple: sausage rolls, smoked salmon sandwiches, turkey soup, warm mince pies, chocolate

Yule log and Christmas cake – the sort of fare they hoped everyone would be ready to devour on a cold winter's night after the nativity play. Kizzie's three older girls had offered to be the waitresses for the night and make sure everyone's glasses and plates were topped up, which would be a great help.

'I've brought masses of fairy lights and scented candles down with me,' Rachel told Bernie and Rosamunde as she stood by the window and lit another cigarette. 'And I have an idea for some entertainment.'

Bernie and Rosamunde exchanged glances. Rachel had some funny ideas about what amounted to entertainment. They'd attended a party at her old flat in London years ago that had involved topless waitresses and bottomless waiters.

'Oh yes?' asked Bernie, weakly.

'You know I've just trained as a teacher of burlesque dance?' she asked. 'Well, I thought I might put on a performance later in the evening. What do you think? It's so glamorous. Honestly, every-one will love it!' Her enthusiasm was so boundless Bernie didn't have the heart to pour cold water over the idea, despite his reservations.

'Sounds marvellous, darling, but will it involve going topless? Only there will be quite a lot of children at the party.' Rachel laughed.

'Of course not, Dad! My own kids will be there, remember! No, no, no. It's a little bit saucy but – I promise – no nudity!'

'Well, I'll be intrigued to see it,' Rosamunde told her sister. 'What's the name of that famous burlesque dancer?'

'Dita Von Teese.'

'That's it. You're quite like her, actually, but with red hair.'

'Oh, I'm far better than her,' Rachel said but instead of sounding arrogant, as she should have done, her confidence was as disarming as usual. Rosamunde threw a cushion at her sister, who laughed and ducked.

Later in the evening the trio were joined by Mrs Garfield and Kizzie, who was looking a little pale and drawn. When they had a moment on their own Rosamunde asked her friend if she was all right.

'Not really,' she said. 'I'm still convinced Gerard's playing away. It's keeping me awake at night.'

'Has anything happened to make you more suspicious?' Rosamunde asked.

'Nothing tangible. Nothing I can confront him with yet. But he's being so shifty and he keeps going out for hours at a time. When I ask where he's been he says he's been seeing his friend John, but he's never had such a close friendship with him before. Why all of a sudden?'

Rosamunde had to admit it was sounding more and more likely, but until there was firm proof, or unless Kizzie confronted her husband, she didn't know how to help.

'Look,' she said. 'Let's get through Christmas and then in the New Year you must talk to him,' she advised her friend. 'Maybe there's a perfectly innocent explanation anyway,' she comforted. Kizzie sighed and pulled herself together, pasting a smile on her face.

'You're right. I'll deal with it after Christmas. Come on; let's get the party sorted for now. I want to hear more about this burlesque dancing,' she giggled.

22.
APRIL 1998

Congratulations!' Kizzie pulled Rosamunde into a hug before grabbing her hand to inspect the ring. 'Beautiful!' she declared. 'I can't believe you're engaged!'

'I know,' grinned Rosamunde. 'Although – and I can only admit this to you – the circumstances weren't exactly ideal.'

'What do you mean?' asked Kizzie as she ordered a bottle of champagne from the bartender. Kizzie had managed to leave the girls with her mother to enjoy a night out in Harbourton with Rosamunde and find out all the juicy details of her engagement.

'Well, you know Giles told me he was taking me away for the weekend?' Kizzie nodded and the pair raised their bubbling glasses to each other. 'Guess where he took me?' Rosamunde continued.

'I give up!' Kizzie replied immediately.

'Jersey!' Rosamunde told her with a grimace.

'Oh hell, what a mistake! I guess he didn't know.'

'Exactly, he didn't, so I could hardly hold it against him, but it was so strange to be there with Giles. Especially as we stayed in the same harbour village as last time. I know it's silly – after all, that was so long ago – but all these memories came back to me and I went into a bit of a decline. Poor Giles couldn't work out what was going on and I didn't want to have to explain it all so I just said I wasn't feeling very well. Anyway, after the first day I pulled myself together and got on with things. When Giles proposed the first thing I felt was relief that he'd done the deed and we could head home again! Isn't that a dreadful thing to admit?'

'Just honest,' replied Kizzie, as she took another sip of champagne. 'And anyway, you said yes, so I'm imagining that – other than his dire choice of proposal destination – you were pleased?'

'Oh, of course! I'd been expecting it, really – it was just a question of when and where. Thankfully he didn't propose in St Aubin. We'd gone to this beautiful five-mile beach in a place called St Ouen and we were walking along the seafront when he suddenly stopped, dropped to his knees and produced a ring. It was very sweet and romantic.'

'Bless him. And when did you get back?'

'Yesterday. Actually, we bumped into Benedict and Clara on the flight home, which was a bit of a coincidence!'

'Oh, of course, I forgot. Her aunt lives there. I think they'd gone over for her cousin's twenty-first birthday party. Were they getting on?' Kizzie asked with a gleam in her eye.

'Well, they seemed to be, but when I told them my news Clara looked very eager. She gave Benedict a lot of meaningful looks. It was quite funny, really! Does he regret getting back together with her, do you think?'

'Who knows with Benedict? I just don't know why he stays with her if he doesn't want to marry her. Goodness only knows, the family would rather he ditched her and found someone new. Oh dear, I've had too much to drink. I'm being a bitch.' Rosamunde laughed and shook her head.

'This is Clara Johnson we're talking about. It would take a saint to be nice about her,' Rosamunde remarked. 'But the champagne's gone straight to my head too. Shall we go through to the restaurant and get something to eat?'

'Good idea. And you can tell me all about the wedding plans.' Inwardly, Rosamunde's heart sank. She was so happy to be engaged to Giles but the prospect of planning a wedding filled her with gloom. Yet somehow she couldn't admit this to anyone. It seemed like some sort of unspoken rule that every woman's dream is to organise a wedding and Rosamunde felt like a freak for not feeling that way.

'I'll tell you what,' said Rosamunde as she and Kizzie took their seats at a table by the window. 'Let's not talk about babies or weddings. Let's pretend we're fourteen again and talk about any old nonsense.'

'You're on,' replied Kizzie, snapping open her menu before whispering to Rosamunde that she should check out the waiter.

'Wow! A definite nine,' whispered back Rosamunde and in a second the girls had reverted to their game of choice at the age of fourteen – scoring boys out of ten. In fact, they'd scored everything out of ten: boys, chips, public lavatories.

'I'm going to the loo,' Rosamunde said a moment later.

'Don't forget to come back with a score,' reminded Kizzie and as Rosamunde wove her way to the ladies she felt lighter than she'd felt in a long time.

23.
FRIDAY 12TH DECEMBER 2014

On a particularly foggy Friday morning Bernie and Rosamunde dispatched Rachel back to London, and they'd just finished waving her off when Mrs Garfield arrived at the Vicarage.

'Ready for our shopping trip?' she asked Rosamunde as she bustled into the cottage.

'All set,' Rosamunde agreed, pulling on her faux-fur coat and grabbing her bag.

'What's this?' asked Bernie, raising his shock of white hair from the newspaper. 'Off to buy some nice frocks?'

'Get away with you!' replied Mrs Garfield. 'Nothing so glamorous. No, we're off to do the big Christmas shop at that huge new supermarket in Totnes. Rosamunde's going to drive,' she said, her eyes wide with awe. Mrs Garfield had passed her driving test but had never driven farther than Thatchley in her life.

'Sounds ghastly,' grimaced Bernie. 'I hope you don't mind if I don't join you? Only I've, erm, got to see a man about a christening,' he declared.

'Liar!' laughed Rosamunde. 'But no, don't worry; we're not going to drag you along with us. You'd be more of a hindrance than a help. Mrs G and I will be done in no time. Just make sure you're here when we get back to help us unload.'

The drive was unpleasant at first, as Rosamunde struggled to see through the fog, but as they left the coast behind them the weather cleared and soon the pair were chattering away about this and that. Within an hour Rosamunde had parked in the enormous car park and the two of them emerged from the Citroën with relief to stretch their cramped limbs.

'Shall we get a coffee first?' asked Rosamunde as she spotted a café at the entrance to the supermarket.

'It'll be getting busy soon,' replied Mrs Garfield. 'Let's get the shop done first and then have a coffee,' she declared and Rosamunde didn't dare argue. They started off by stocking up on the alcohol they would need for Christmas itself (the party drink having already been dealt with) and soon they were stuffing crisps, nuts and chocolate into the trolley along with any other goods they could possibly need that would still be in date by Christmas. They would buy the vegetables and other fresh produce from the village nearer the time and the turkey had been ordered from a butcher in Thatchley.

At the bakery, Mrs Garfield tutted at the price of cakes and other baked goods.

'Why don't people do their own baking?' she asked. 'Far cheaper and twice the taste,' she muttered.

'Not everyone's as good at it as you,' Rosamunde chuckled. 'I've been living off shop-bought cakes for the last fifteen years. I'd forgotten how delicious your homemade ones are,' she said, squeezing Mrs Garfield around the shoulders. Mrs G continued to tut but looked pleased with the compliment nonetheless.

By eleven thirty they had stashed the bulging carrier bags and boxes into every conceivable corner of the car and decided that rather than have their coffee at the shopping complex – which was by now heaving – they would head into Totnes to find a slightly less mobbed place to sit down.

It proved harder than they'd hoped, though, as the whole of Totnes seemed to be out and about, stocking up for Christmas and taking well-earned breaks in the various coffee houses. But finally Rosamunde spotted a cosy-looking venue with a spare table at the steamy window. They were about to dash in to claim it when suddenly Rosamunde spotted Gerard across the street.

'Hey, Gerard!' she called loudly, but he hurried along without looking back. 'That was Gerard, wasn't it?' Rosamunde asked, turning to Mrs Garfield.

'Looked a bit like him, but it can't have been or he'd have stopped,' she replied. 'Now come on, before someone else takes that table.' Mrs Garfield hurried into the warmth of the café with a bemused Rosamunde following behind. She was sure it was Gerard she'd just seen, but perhaps he hadn't heard her. And soon enough her mind was on other matters.

'Oooh, hot chocolate,' said Mrs Garfield as she looked at the laminated menu. Rosamunde's mouth watered at the prospect.

'Two mugs of cocoa, please,' she asked the waitress a moment later and soon the two women were engrossed in a conversation about Mrs Croft from the village, who was treating her daughter's wedding as though it were her own.

'Control freak,' said Mrs Garfield, knowledgeably. 'There was a woman like that on *Jeremy Kyle* the other day – controlled her daughter's every move even though she was nearly forty!' Rosamunde sank back in her chair, took a sip and relished another gossipy instalment from dear old Mrs G.

24.
SUMMER 1999

It was just over two weeks until the wedding and Rosamunde was starting to panic that she hadn't yet found a dress. Rachel was calling her daily, trying to persuade her to make a visit to London. To Rachel, Rosamunde was a complete enigma: if she'd been getting married the dress would have been first on her list of priorities.

On a Thursday morning she was in the dentist's waiting room when she came upon a copy of *OK!* magazine, which was featuring the wedding of Posh Spice and David Beckham. She leafed through the article, agog at the organisation that must have gone into their wedding – though presumably they could afford a planner, lucky devils – and by the time she'd finished, she knew she must take action. After a busy afternoon at work, Rosamunde called her sister.

'Rach, are you free tomorrow? Can you help me find a wedding dress?'

'Is the Pope a Catholic?' Rachel replied. 'I've got to work in the morning but I'll be done by lunchtime – bloody actors won't work on a Friday afternoon anyway. I'll meet you at Harrods at two thirty.' Rachel was currently working as a make-up artist on the set of a BBC production of *Mansfield Park* (much to Kizzie's excitement) and was always full of interesting gossip, most of it gleaned in pillow-talk from one or other of the actors. She was currently enjoying a dalliance with the actor playing Edmund and Rosamunde had to admit she was more than a little envious.

It was a steaming hot July day and Rosamunde arrived at Harrods feeling decidedly over-heated. There were few things she felt like doing less than trying on wedding dresses and her task was made even harder by the fact she needed a gown that was *prêt-à-porter* as there was no time for it to be altered to fit her or, less still, made from scratch. Still, with Rachel's help, by six o'clock that evening Rosamunde had selected a beautiful, simple dress made of white silk. It had a princess neckline and sashayed beautifully as she walked. She'd shied away from all the meringues that filled the bridal suite and had opted for one of the few unfussy dresses that were available. When she'd seen herself in the mirror Rosamunde had gasped; it was so strange to see herself in a long, white dress. Rachel was uncharacteristically quiet.

'Shit, Rosamunde,' she said. 'Mum would have been so proud.'

The mention of their mother seemed to raise her spirit immediately. It was as though she was suddenly in the room with them, sat on the *chaise longue* with her serene smile and her impish haircut.

Rosamunde had always believed in ghosts but had never before seen or even felt the presence of one. But a moment later she felt absolutely certain her mother was standing beside her. She closed her eyes and felt her mum stroke her long hair; it was such a gentle sensation that she felt the hairs on the back of her neck stand up and a soporific feeling wash over her. Rosamunde willed her mother to say something. To tell her she was doing the right thing. That she was proud of her. She knew her mother must have been there for a reason.

'Is everything okay?' asked the timid sales assistant, entering the changing area to find two silent women and a ghost. Unwittingly she had broken the spell. Rosamunde felt her mother disappear immediately.

'Fine,' she had smiled. 'We'll get this one.'

Now, with the wedding dress bundled into a bag and sitting between them in the taxi, the girls decided to treat themselves to a cocktail or two and dinner out. Thanks to Rachel's television contacts, she was a member of The Groucho Club in Soho and so, as soon as Rachel had signed in her sister and stashed the wedding dress in a locker, they entered the sultry glamour of the elite club for creatives.

They started with cocktails at the ground floor bar where Rosamunde found herself barely able to concentrate on her sister as she sipped on her White Russian and star-gazed – on Friday nights the club was always brimming with celebrities. In the end Rachel dragged Rosamunde through to the leather banquettes of the downstairs eating area where they ordered burgers and a decent bottle of red.

'So please tell me the rest of the wedding is better organised than the dress buying. I'm sorry I've been so useless at helping get things sorted but work's been crazy,' Rachel said, taking a large slurp of wine. Rosamunde considered for a moment, thinking of the 'to-do' list she had slowly worked through, from arranging the church service (easy enough), to selecting a venue for the reception (harder) and deciding on a menu that was both affordable and interesting (impossible).

'It's fine, actually – all arranged. I must admit I haven't enjoyed the preparations as much as I feel I should have done. I guess I'm just not a natural bride.'

Rachel scrutinised her sister carefully. 'Are you sure you're doing the right thing here, Rosamunde? You do love Giles, right?'

'Of course I do.' Rosamunde was quick to answer this. She had no doubt. It was just the thought of the wedding that fazed her. She'd never been a great one for attention.

'Good. Look, I know you think I'd be busting to be centre of attention if it were my big day but even I would feel nervous, so don't give yourself a hard time. Now come on, spill the beans. I want to know all the details.'

By the time they'd finished their burgers and Rosamunde had woven her way up the narrow staircase to the bathroom she was feeling much more excited about her impending nuptials. As she washed her hands in the small washroom she studied herself in the mirror. Her hair was looking glossy and smooth, her amber eyes looked bright and her skin had just the right amount of wine-induced glow about it.

'Rosamunde Pemberton, soon you'll be a married woman,' she told herself, testing the reaction. She felt happy. Contented.

As she headed back to the restaurant Rosamunde found herself stumbling slightly down the three steps that led to the landing below. A helpful gentleman reached out his arm to steady her. She looked up, slightly embarrassed but grateful. The man smiled for a moment and then frowned.

As Rosamunde fainted all she could see was the colour turquoise.

25.
SATURDAY 13TH DECEMBER 2014

It was now a week and a half until Christmas and Rosamunde knew she could no longer put off the task of buying the rest of her Christmas presents. She bundled herself into her coat and was about to climb into Bernie's car when she suddenly decided she would save the shopping until the afternoon when the light would dim and she could fully enjoy the sight of Thatchley illuminated for Christmas. In the meantime she would wander down to the church hall to see how the nativity play rehearsals were getting on.

The heating had now been fixed but on this particularly cold winter's day Rosamunde kept her coat on as she sat at the back of the hall and watched her father's attempts at directing his chaotic cast. Florence and Anna sat serenely enough in the stable with Baby Henry in Anna's arms (she was playing Mary as her hair was longer), but the shepherds appeared to be engrossed in a conversation with the innkeeper, appropriately enough about the new ale the landlord of The Dragon's Head had recently started to serve, and were oblivious to Bernie's appeals to listen to him. Meanwhile, the angels were squabbling about the fact the Angel Gabriel kept bossing them around (that was Harriet for you) and the three kings were slouched on the side of the stage looking glum. Rosamunde supposed they

had better things to do with their Saturday morning. She was about
to intervene when suddenly a ferocious bellowing made her jump.

'Will everyone please shut up!'

All heads turned to see the source of this almost godly voice.

'Thank you,' the voice continued as its owner emerged from the
corridor into the main hall. It was Benedict.

'Listen, everyone, we had this conversation the other day. The
more noise you all make when Bernie's trying to direct, the longer
the rehearsals will take. So please, let's just get on with it.'

After delivering his speech Benedict headed to the back of the
hall and it was only then he spotted Rosamunde.

'Oh,' he cringed. 'I didn't realise you were here!'

'Oh, don't be embarrassed,' Rosamunde told him. 'I'm impressed.
I've never seen you so authoritative.'

'I popped in the other day and saw them all running rings
round poor Bernie,' Benedict explained. 'Goodness knows what it'll
be like when he has to direct the animals as well. Anyway, I decided
to step in and help him out. I'm loud when I need to be.'

'You are indeed,' replied Rosamunde, in awe of this side of
Benedict she'd never seen before. Then she heard another loud
noise – a grumbling stomach.

'Hungry?' she asked, smiling.

'Ravenous.'

'Let's get some lunch at The Kiln. My shout,' said Rosamunde
as she gathered up her bag.

Outside the hall, Rosamunde was met with a bouncing greet-
ing from Humphrey, who was tied to the railings and seemed very
relieved he hadn't been abandoned there forever. At The Kiln,
however, the poor mutt had to be tied up outside again. He looked
suitably hangdog.

'It's not for long, old chap,' Benedict told him before grabbing
Rosamunde's hand and dragging her into the steamy café. After

ordering some soup, Rosamunde found herself observing Benedict with curiosity.

'It is odd,' she told him.

'What's odd?' asked Benedict. 'Other than you, of course.'

'Just how little I knew you until now, even though I've known you all my life.'

'Well, in fairness you only really knew me as a kid and by my own admission I was seriously annoying. I grew out of that by the time I went to college, but by then you'd totally written me off.' He grinned ruefully.

'You're probably right. Why *were* you so annoying?'

'Some kids are, I guess,' Benedict shrugged. 'And I've always been naturally clumsy, which is inevitably irritating. If I was inter-rogated by a psychiatrist I might at a push say I was lacking in confidence thanks to my high-achieving and perfectly conform-ing elder sister, but I don't think it's fair to blame her for my imperfections.'

'Oh, you're not so imperfect,' chuckled Rosamunde. 'And in any event, who am I to judge? I certainly don't fall into Kizzie's camp.'

'That you don't,' confirmed Benedict. 'But I love you for it. It makes me feel so much better,' he ribbed her. 'Now, enough of this idle chit-chat. What are we doing this afternoon?'

Rosamunde's peaceful trip to Thatchley was thus quickly transformed into a less quiet but much more fun-filled visit with Benedict and Humphrey at her side. Just trying to make their way along the high street proved difficult, with every other person enchanted by Humphrey and stopping to fuss over him, though Rosamunde noted most of them were female and she suspected Benedict might be just as much of a draw. She chuckled inwardly at their futile attempts at attracting his attention. One particular woman was incredibly pretty but she was left as disappointed as the rest.

The lights were just as captivating as Rosamunde had hoped they'd be, and as they moved slowly along the high street she rubbernecked, taking in all the magical illuminations and pausing now and then to point out a particularly imaginative arrangement.

'You're so cute,' Benedict told her. 'Just like a big kid.'

'Don't forget, I've not had a Christmas at home for fifteen years. I'd forgotten how utterly thrilling the whole lead-up is. Come on, let's head to the square and see if the carol singers have started.'

They had indeed, and they were delightful. Benedict bought himself and Rosamunde each a small beaker of mulled wine. They cradled their drinks as they watched the singers, joining in with the well-known carols until Benedict's off-key voice seemed to perturb Humphrey and he began to howl, making the whole square turn to them and chuckle.

'I've told you before about your voice,' Rosamunde teased as they scurried off with Humphrey, who was now in danger of upstaging the carol singers.

Next they hit the shops, which were crammed with stressed-looking shoppers who were red-faced from the contrast between the icy afternoon outside and the excessive heating of the stores' interiors. With Benedict's help Rosamunde quickly bought the remaining presents she needed and it was just as they were heading back to the car that she had a thought.

'You know what? There's one person I've forgotten to put on my list,' she told Benedict.

'Who?' he asked.

'You,' Rosamunde said. 'I think you've earned your stripes. Is there anything particular you'd like?'

'Gosh, I'm honoured,' Benedict replied with a wry smile. 'Probably some ski socks,' he told her. 'Very useful.' Rosamunde laughed.

'It may be cold at the moment, but ski socks?'

'Not for here,' he explained. 'A friend of mine owns a ski chalet in Chamonix and it's free for the whole of January, so he's letting it to me for a month at a knockdown price. I leave on Boxing Day.'

'You do?' Rosamunde felt unaccountably disappointed. 'What about Humphrey?' she asked.

'He's coming with me in the Land Rover – I'm getting the ferry and driving down. You look as though your fiancé just told you he was leaving you for another woman,' he smiled. 'I'm flattered!'

Rosamunde dug him in the ribs. 'I'm just surprised,' she told him. 'You haven't mentioned it before. And I admit, I'll miss you. Maybe I need to make some more friends. It'll be a long month without you,' she admitted grudgingly.

'Well, I'm here for now,' he told her. 'So let's have some fun. How about I come round to yours tonight for a game of Scrabble?'

'Such a fabulous sense of fun!' Rosamunde laughed.

But in the event it was a wonderfully festive evening. When they arrived back at the Vicarage they encountered the delicious scent of roasting chicken coming from the Aga. They deposited Humphrey in the sitting room; he was exhausted from their excursion and immediately hogged the hearth rug, much to Gladys's disgust. They went in search of Bernie and (presumably) Mrs Garfield and tracked them down in the attic.

'We're back!' Rosamunde shouted up from the base of the ladder into the dark hole above. 'What are you doing?'

Immediately Mrs Garfield's face appeared through the hole. 'Oh, hello, dears. Bernie's searching for the Christmas decorations. We thought it was about time we put them up.'

'Oh yes!' Rosamunde bounced up and down with excitement. 'Can I put the angel on the top of the tree?'

Benedict raised his dark eyebrows at her and shook his head in despair, but later, after a merry supper, he happily joined in with the decorating. The Christmas tree (which was far too large for the sitting room) was decked with a mishmash of decorations, most of them bought with love by Marguerite when the children were small. She was responsible for the girls' continuing excitement about the festive season, so enthusiastic was she every year as Christmas approached.

Benedict carefully arranged the nativity scene on the mantelpiece and when he discovered the Baby Jesus's head was missing he found some glue and patiently set about fixing the figure at the kitchen table while Mrs Garfield made hot chocolate. When they re-joined the others in the sitting room, Bernie and Mrs Garfield were tasked with disentangling and arranging the fairy lights on the tree and, as she had requested, Rosamunde was granted the honour of placing the charmingly tatty angel on top of the tree with Benedict's assistance.

They were too exhausted for Scrabble but it had been a day and evening of fun and wonder, made all the more magical for it being Rosamunde's first English Christmas in years. Yet at the outskirts of her mind she could feel the tug of little threads of disturbance. As she lay in the old-fashioned bathtub before bed she tried to place these strands of concern. What could she possibly feel troubled about after such a perfect day? Before she could analyse the latent problem further, Rosamunde pulled herself out of the steaming water and wrapped herself in a soft towel. *Tomorrow*, she told herself. *I'll think about it tomorrow.*

26.
JULY 1999

Rosamunde was stone cold with shock. She was sitting on the sofa in Rachel's flat on Adam Street with a blanket wrapped round her as Stephen crouched on the floor in front of her, his turquoise eyes full of concern.

'Here, drink this,' he ordered, handing her a brandy. Rachel had gone to bed, unusually tactful in the midst of this spectacular event.

'You're married,' she said, immediately spotting the wedding ring on Stephen's left hand. He shrugged apologetically.

'You'd better tell me what happened,' Rosamunde told him, as her heart raced. It was amazing, she thought, how her heart's memory was so sharp. At the very sight of Stephen it had reverted to its unsteady pound when for twelve years it had rarely skipped a beat.

'I need you to know, there was no deceit on my part,' Stephen told her earnestly. 'God knows I'd throttle my grandmother if she were still alive.'

'Your grandmother?' Rosamunde asked, confused. And so the story unfolded. It transpired that, while Stephen's parents had drowned in the Zeebrugge disaster, Stephen had been rescued. After a spell in hospital recovering from a head injury, he was returned to his grandmother in Reading, but as soon as he stepped into the safety of her arms his whole mind and body had shut down in shock and grief. He was suffering with post-traumatic stress disorder (a fairly new diagnosis at the time) and while his body soon recovered, his memory was left impaired for years to come. He suffered amnesia and doctors couldn't be certain to what degree it had been caused by the head injury or the stress. He remembered nothing of his life before it had been changed forever by the tragedy on the MS *Herald of Free Enterprise*. As a result, he'd been unable to remember Rosamunde.

'But your gran knew about me.' Rosamunde's head was a whirl of confusion. 'Why didn't she tell you?'

'I've asked myself the same question for the last three years, since memories have started to come back to me. Gran died about five years ago so I was never able to ask her. I think the bottom line was my gran was devastated by the loss of her son piled on top of losing my sister all those years ago and so she hung on to me for dear life. I guess she knew how serious we were about each other back then and thought that if she told me about you I'd be bound to pick up with you where we left off. I think she was worried I'd leave home to be with you. Which, in all fairness, I probably would have done.' He smiled, his dimples as prominent as they'd always been. Rosamunde drank him in: that smile, the eyes, both features so unchanged, and yet his blond hair had receded slightly and his body, while not fat, had bulked out.

'But other people – your friends – you must have told them about me,' Rosamunde pointed out.

'I think my grandmother must have called around and told everyone not to talk about anything that had happened before the disaster. I remember feeling incredibly isolated in the months that followed – it was horrendous knowing I was supposedly friends with these people. But we shared no history, and whenever I asked them to remind me about things they were wary. They certainly never mentioned you.'

'But what about when the memories started to come back? What happened then?' asked Rosamunde, visibly distressed. Stephen sighed.

'There's a lot to explain,' he said. 'Look, it's late and there's so much to discuss. I'm going to head home. How about we meet up tomorrow? I could pick you up at noon and take you somewhere for lunch?' he asked. Rosamunde, still in a daze of shock, agreed, though really she wanted him to stay all night. Not just to explain everything to her, but to kiss her, to take her to bed, to devour her. Then she stopped herself. Stephen was married. Even if he wanted to devour her – which clearly he didn't – she could never bring herself to be the other woman. It wasn't the sort of person she was. And then, of course, there was Giles.

❧

The next day, after a fitful sleep, Rosamunde took great care getting ready for their lunch appointment. She may have decided to put her head very firmly in charge of her heart but she still wanted to look good for the occasion, not least to feel she had some sort of control when in fact she felt as though she were unravelling like a snagged garment. She was supposed to be returning to Harbourton this morning but she rang Giles and briefly told him she'd decided to spend an extra night with her sister. Poor Giles was of course obliging about the change of plans.

'You haven't changed at all,' Stephen told Rosamunde as she opened the door to him. Again, her treacherous heart began to hammer. *Deep breaths*, she told herself. *Deep breaths*.

Rosamunde had expected lunch in a nearby wine bar but Stephen had his car parked outside and it soon became clear he was driving them out of London. They drove in silence, in tacit agreement they both needed a drink to help them through this. Finally they arrived at a beautiful thatched pub in a remote country village where they found themselves an outdoor table in the corner of the beer garden, far away from the cheerful weekend drinkers. Rosamunde sat nervously at the picnic bench and Stephen ordered them beers and brought them out, his hands remarkably steady as he wove his way to Rosamunde.

'How are you, babe?' Stephen asked as he sat down and Rosamunde, noting Stephen's old term of endearment for her, thought it was a question she wouldn't know where to begin to answer.

'Is life good?' he continued. Rosamunde hesitated.

'It is. It was. I'm getting married in two weeks' time.'

'Congratulations!' Stephen exclaimed, though his jaw looked tense.

'Cut to the chase, Stephen, please,' begged Rosamunde. She needed this over with. She needed to know and then she needed to move on with her life.

'Of course,' he answered, his voice soft and understanding.

So Stephen explained. He and Jodie – his wife of five years (*five years!*) – were holidaying in the West Country three years ago when he'd started to get weird flashbacks during a day trip to Thatchley. By the end of the holiday he'd remembered everything and found himself sending his bewildered wife back to London while he remained in Devon for another week, working through the memories and deciding what to do next.

He had stayed in Thatchley at The Three Bells and every day he'd almost made the short trip to Potter's Cove to see if Bernie and Rosamunde were still living at the Vicarage. But he never did. After agonising about it every day for a week he had returned to London. He had made a life for himself and he imagined Rosamunde had too. He'd determined to leave the past behind him. He was happy with the life he had in London. He liked his job. He loved his wife. Their marriage wasn't perfect – it had its ups and downs – but he knew if he'd returned to Potter's Cove he would have unpeeled a layer of himself with potentially disastrous consequences for everyone.

Rosamunde thought back to what she had been doing three years ago. She'd been living in Harbourton, working where she worked now and without a fiancé or even a boyfriend. She wondered if her father would have told her if Stephen had paid him a visit. Of course he would have. And it was true: it would have shocked her then as it had shaken her to the core right now. But Rosamunde felt cheated. She was angry that Stephen had allowed her to continue thinking he was dead when he was very much alive.

'I grieved for you, Stephen. I grieved for you so badly.'

Stephen looked suitably apologetic. 'I'm so sorry, babe, but I truly didn't remember a thing until that holiday in the West Country and I assumed you would have been well and truly over me by then.'

It occurred to Rosamunde, then, that of course he knew nothing about the aftermath of his supposed death.

'I was pregnant, you know,' she told him, and watched as Stephen's tanned face immediately paled.

'No way! I never thought. How stupid – it never even occurred to me. I'm a father!' he exclaimed. 'A boy or a girl?' he asked. 'They must be, what, twelve by now?' Stephen had gone from shocked to excited in a moment. Rosamunde shook her head.

'I lost the baby,' she told him, and even now the memories squeezed her heart uncomfortably.

'Shit,' Stephen replied, evidently crushed. 'Wow, I really thought I might be a father for a moment there. There's nothing I'd have loved more.'

'You don't have kids with Jodie then?' Rosamunde asked, the name sticking in her throat. Stephen shook his head.

'We've been trying for years – we're both desperate for them – but we're not having much luck. Jodie's keen for us to try IVF but I don't know . . .' He tailed off, as though he couldn't begin to deal with his current troubles when the past had now reared its ugly head in such an astonishing fashion.

'I wish I could have been there for you when you lost the baby,' Stephen said as he reached over to stroke Rosamunde's hand. A moment later, without a word, they both stood up. As they walked towards the car Rosamunde's arm brushed against Stephen's and in an instant he grabbed hold of her. There wasn't a moment of hesitation before the two were entwined in an embrace the likes of which Rosamunde had forgotten existed. She hated herself for it but her heart had stealthily crept up on her head, knocked it out and taken over.

27.
SUNDAY 14TH DECEMBER 2014

It was the day of the annual Christingle service, an event that marked the real countdown to Christmas as far as the village was concerned. It took place at four o'clock in the afternoon when darkness had descended, and the churchwardens painstakingly lit all the candles around the church so the service could take place in candlelight alone.

It was a heart-warming service, if a little nerve-wracking, as all the small children of the village processed around the church holding oranges bearing lit votives. The possibility of the children setting each other on fire seemed rather high, even with the vigilance of anxious parents, but each year the service had gone remarkably without incident. This one was no exception, and Bernie breathed an audible sigh of relief as each child was asked to blow out their candle at the end of the service.

Rosamunde was sitting with Kizzie, Gerard and the five girls, and it was only when she turned around towards the end of the service that she saw that Benedict was behind her with another man. Immediately she assumed he had a new boyfriend, although she was surprised he hadn't mentioned this piece of news to her.

'Who's the guy with Benedict?' she whispered to Kizzie.

'Gorgeous, isn't he?' she replied. 'An old friend of his. Divorced and, as far as I'm aware, not gay. I think he likes the look of you,' she nudged. It was true that he seemed to be looking enquiringly in their direction before whispering to Benedict. Rosamunde turned quickly around.

As they trooped slowly out of the church Benedict and his friend caught up with her.

'Rosamunde, allow me to introduce you to my old mate Ed,' Benedict announced. 'Ed, this is Rosamunde. Rosamunde, this is Ed Baker. He's staying with me for Christmas.'

She looked up at the very distinguished-looking man who had friendly, crinkly eyes with a gleam in them and a firm handshake. Rosamunde placed him as a little older than her and wondered how Benedict knew him.

'Good to meet you,' he said. 'Are you coming back to Benedict's for supper?' he asked.

'Oh, well, I . . .' Rosamunde faltered.

'You are invited.' Benedict grinned. 'I meant to ask you yesterday but I forgot. Thought it was about time I returned some of your hospitality. Can you remember how to get there?'

༄

It had been many years since Rosamunde had visited Farm Cottage, a small house on the farmland owned by Kizzie and Benedict's parents. An old farm worker had lived there with his wife when Rosamunde was a child, but now it had been taken over by Benedict and turned into a veritable bachelor pad. As she knocked on the door she heard Humphrey attempting his impression of a guard dog (rather half-heartedly, she thought) before Ed welcomed her in. The smell of garlic and chilli assaulted her as she walked through the door and immediately her mouth watered.

'You can cook?' she asked Benedict, astonished, remembering the half-cooked buns at the Tiny Tots' Christmas party.

'Certainly not,' Ed told her. 'But I'm not bad at rustling up the odd dish. Could be a bit spicy. Hope you're okay with that?'

'I love a bit of spice,' Rosamunde told him, giggling. Was she flirting? Benedict looked at them and she couldn't tell if he was annoyed or pleased.

'Well, come on in, then,' he told her. 'Let's get you a drink.'

A very pleasant evening ensued and Rosamunde was given a tour of the house, which was tidy but not fastidiously so. The tour included Benedict's studio, where she noticed a work in progress.

'You've been inspired?' she asked.

'I don't want to jinx it,' said Benedict. 'But yes, my inspiration seems finally to be returning. I'm working on this vase for Mrs G. I just need to finish painting it. What do you think so far?'

Rosamunde found it touching he was making a Christmas present for Mrs Garfield and was suitably impressed with the vase, which was a bright shade of Mediterranean sky blue. She remembered Kizzie saying Benedict's signature style was the vibrant colours of his pots. As she looked at some of his older pieces she found herself imagining Benedict living in some beautiful villa in the hills of Mallorca, working diligently as sun shone through into his workshop. The brightly coloured objects seemed such a contrast to the cold and damp of the West Country at this time of year, but then perhaps just working on the pots was enough to lift his spirits.

As the evening drew on, Rosamunde felt at ease with Benedict's friend, who was warm and charming. It turned out the men had been friends since Benedict's car accident, which had happened when he was twenty-five. Ed, an ex–army officer, was driving the truck that collided with Benedict's car on a dark, wet night and following the accident the men had formed an unlikely friendship.

Ed had been wracked with guilt and had arranged for an army physiotherapist, who helped rehabilitate wounded soldiers, to work with Benedict. Thanks to the excellent treatment, Benedict had managed to get rid of the limp he'd been left with after his complex fracture, and now the only legacy of the accident was some lingering back pain, which flared up every now and again.

'What do you do now you're retired from the army?' Rosamunde asked Ed over supper.

'I was in the Veterinary Corps so I work as a vet nowadays,' he explained. 'It's very different now I'm working with farm animals, but I love it and it means I get to live in the country. Can't stand cities. I do visit London once a month, though, to see the children. I'm divorced,' he added, as he looked Rosamunde squarely in the eye.

Rosamunde thought, quite simply, that a more eligible man for her could not exist. What's more, it was clear he was interested. But was she? Could she finally find it in herself to unfurl her heart again? She certainly found Ed attractive and when she kissed his cheek goodnight he smelt wonderful. But then she kissed Benedict. And, to her surprise, he smelt even better.

28.
JULY 1999

For the next twenty-four hours Rosamunde enjoyed an intense journey of re-discovery, banishing worry and guilt from her mind as she and Stephen explored every inch of each other anew in a pretty hotel room in Sussex.

There were new discoveries – how did Stephen get that scar on his leg? – as well as old habits, such as Rosamunde falling asleep in the nook of Stephen's neck as she'd done twelve years before. There were also some disappointments.

'Are you working on a movie at the moment?' Rosamunde asked as they lay in each other's arms.

'What?' queried Stephen, confused. Rosamunde rolled onto her side to look at him.

'You're a film director, right?' she asked. Stephen laughed.

'I'm sorry to disappoint you, babe, but I'm an accountant. I had amnesia, remember? It was only a couple of years ago that I recalled how fervently I'd wanted to direct movies. Bit late to change career direction now and anyway, don't tell anyone, but I quite like my job,' he stage-whispered. 'A friend of mine works in film, though. That's why I was at The Groucho the other night,' he explained.

Rosamunde was disappointed. She'd always thought he'd have followed his dreams if he'd survived, but then she could hardly blame him for not doing so when he couldn't even remember them. How she hated his grandmother at that moment when she thought of all the dreams she'd prevented Stephen from realising for such selfish reasons. *And my life too,* Rosamunde screamed inwardly. *You've messed up my life, too, you stupid old bag!* And yet, had she really ruined Rosamunde's life? Yes, it was hard all those years ago but she had Giles now. She was about to marry him. Wasn't she happy? Rosamunde pushed these thoughts away and allowed her lips to seek out Stephen's.

However, when Stephen dropped her back at Rachel's flat the following day, they were forced to consider what to do next.

'What now?' asked Rosamunde, turning to him from the passenger seat. Stephen sighed.

'I can't be without you, babe,' he told her. He didn't need to ask Rosamunde to know she felt the same. 'Look, how about I get some time off work and come down to see you? We need to formulate a plan before we tell Jodie and what's-his-face.'

'Giles,' Rosamunde told him, prickling. She might have been about to shatter Giles's heart, but he deserved to be called by his proper name.

'Sorry. Giles. What do you say?'

Rosamunde could hardly think straight but she agreed. After a lingering kiss, she dragged herself out of the car, barely able to tear herself away, and ran up the steps to her sister's flat where Rachel was waiting with the lack of judgement and glut of comfort only a sister can provide.

Later that day, Rosamunde returned home to find Giles working on her computer at the desk in the small sitting room. As soon as she entered the flat she felt both guilty and oppressed. She rushed to the window to let some air in.

'Good trip?' asked Giles, looking up briefly from his work. 'Where's the dress?'

Rosamunde realised, in horror, that she had forgotten about it entirely and the gown was at this moment hanging in her sister's wardrobe. 'Oh, I left it at Rachel's so you wouldn't see it. She's bringing it down before the wedding,' she told him, ashamed at how easily the lies were pouring from her tongue. She realised quite quickly that she couldn't cope with having Giles in the flat right now and so she feigned a bad migraine and sent him back to his bachelor pad, telling him she'd see him tomorrow.

'It's probably down to pre-wedding stress,' he told her, concerned. 'Make sure you get lots of rest, now, won't you?' he bossed, solicitous. Rosamunde wished he would stop fussing but promised she would.

Having despatched him from the flat, she turned and rested against the inside of the door, before sliding down it with a sigh of relief, exhaustion and despair. Her sister would be better at this, she thought, and she wondered for a moment if Stephen was worth the heartbreak and upset she was about to cause. But her doubt didn't last long: when she brought the image of him into her mind she found herself immediately revived from her exhausted stupor. She loved him with a fervour that both excited and terrified her and when he arrived unexpectedly an hour later, unable to be apart from her for any longer (and, presumably, after making excuses to Jodie), she succumbed to their bubble of bliss for another twenty-four hours.

During this time, while holed up in Rosamunde's tiny flat, they decided they must tell Jodie and Giles as soon as possible. It wasn't fair to drag this out.

Rosamunde and Giles had arranged to meet at the Vicarage the following evening for their rather late-in-the-proceedings wedding interview with Bernie to discuss the finer details of the service. He'd had a run of weddings and his daughter's had been put to the bottom of the pile. And so Rosamunde decided she would bite the bullet and explain everything to Giles then. Stephen, meanwhile, would return to London and start the process of separation and divorce with Jodie. The prospect of the days ahead was miserable but Rosamunde and Stephen were resolute. They'd never been so certain about anything in their lives.

It was thus that Rosamunde found herself arriving at the Vicarage on a beautiful summer's evening to find Bernie and Giles sitting in the garden drinking Pimm's. The scene was so perfect she felt like a vandal about to smash an exquisite piece of artwork. So she stood frozen by the garden gate until Gladys gave her away as she bundled towards Rosamunde with a loud *miaow*.

When Giles saw her he stood up to embrace her, smiling, but as soon as he took in her face he sat down again with a thump. It was as if, in that moment, he absolutely knew, although nothing whatsoever had been said. Bernie made himself scarce and the next two hours were full of painful explanations, sad pleadings from Giles and heart-wrenching tears. By ten o'clock Giles had left and Rosamunde, though by now shivering from the evening chill and the trauma of the last couple of hours, remained rooted to the garden chair. When Bernie emerged with a warm cardigan and a glass of brandy, asking no questions but giving her a brief squeeze, she was unspeakably grateful.

'Poor Giles,' she said.

'Better now than later,' replied Bernie, always a wise old owl.

She had done it. The next few days would have to be spent unscrambling the wedding plans but she began to feel a weak sense of relief that there need be no more lies. No more deceit. It was all out in the open, however devastating.

Most of all, Rosamunde felt relieved that she and Stephen were edging slowly closer to being together again – at last.

29.
MONDAY 15TH DECEMBER 2014

When Rosamunde bumped into Benedict in the newsagent's on Monday morning he looked terribly gloomy.

'Why the long face?' she asked, as she grabbed a carton of milk from the fridge.

'Guess who's back in Potter's Cove for Christmas?' Benedict answered. He didn't pause before continuing, with a grimace, 'Clara.'

'Oh dear,' replied Rosamunde, with a sympathetic smile. This was the trouble with growing up in a small village. There were some ghosts that haunted you forever. 'Have you seen her?'

'No, I just bumped into Bob the postman and he told me he saw her arriving at her parents' house early this morning with her husband and baby. What am I going to do?'

'What you are going to do,' Rosamunde ordered him, 'is not allow her to ruin your Christmas. Anyway, she's got what she wanted – she has a husband and baby now. She'll probably be all sweetness and light.'

Rosamunde was mistaken. Later the same day she came across Clara outside The Kiln. Rosamunde spotted her a moment before she was seen herself and contemplated ducking into the café to avoid any conversation before deciding to be brave.

'Well, well,' came the whiney voice. 'Rosamunde Pemberton!' she announced. 'Or maybe you have a new surname by now? Are you married?' she asked, getting straight to the point.

'Hi, Clara,' Rosamunde replied, doing her best to be friendly. 'And no, not married.' Clara put on her faux-sympathetic face.

'Oh, really? That's a shame. I thought you might have found someone else by now, after all that business with that chap. What was his name? Giles?'

'That's right, but no,' Rosamunde replied with a tight smile. Clara wasn't holding back. The irritating woman took a moment to coo at the baby on her hip. The infant looked much like her – sort of blonde and horsey, with freckles.

'How about children?' Clara demanded to know next.

'Again, no,' Rosamunde answered. She was sure her voice must sound strangled. Clara couldn't even manage faux sympathy now. She just looked gleeful, as if she'd won some sort of race Rosamunde had no idea she was participating in.

'This is Hugo,' she told Rosamunde proudly. 'And his daddy's name is Rupert. I'm sure you'll meet him over the next few days. We're down until Boxing Day,' she said brightly.

'Great,' Rosamunde managed before spotting Benedict taking Humphrey for a walk down to Inner Cove. 'Better get on but lovely to see you, Clara,' she lied before scuttling off in Benedict's direction so she could warn him to steer clear.

By the time she drew near him she was out of breath.

'Benedict, wait!' she shouted. He walked terribly fast. He turned around and, as he did so, she suddenly found her remaining breath taken from her as she took in – as if for the first time – his distinct jaw line and beautiful Roman nose. When he saw it was Rosamunde he smiled, and his large dark eyes crinkled with friendliness. *Oh no*, Rosamunde thought to herself. Suddenly her anxiety in the bath the other night made sense to her. How had she not realised this before? She despaired inwardly. Only she would find herself falling in love with a man who was gay. She could cry at the ineptitude of her pitiful heart.

'Are you okay?' Benedict asked, rushing towards her as Humphrey gambolled along beside him. 'You've gone quite white,' he said. Rosamunde shook herself mentally and physically.

'Fine.' She grinned. 'Someone walked over my grave, that's all.' He looked puzzled.

'You know,' she said. 'When you get that weird shiver down your back.'

'Crazy lady,' Benedict declared with a grin as he hugged her to him. As Rosamunde looked up over his shoulder she saw a figure on the slipway looking down at them.

'Let go, quick,' Rosamunde ordered and, confused, Benedict did so.

'What?' he asked.

'Oh, she's gone again,' replied Rosamunde. 'It was Clara. We don't want her thinking you're heterosexual again,' she laughed.

'No,' Benedict said gravely. 'That we definitely don't. Still, she'd never think we were a couple,' he added. 'So I think we're safe.'

Rosamunde felt hurt, but she bit her lip and they walked on together along the damp sand, their noses pink on this icy December day. Rosamunde decided to change the topic of conversation.

'How's Ed getting on?' she asked.

'Good,' Benedict replied. 'He's a fabulous guest. No trouble at all. He seems to be rather taken with you,' he added.

'Really?' Rosamunde decided to be modest, though really it would have been impossible not to have noticed.

'Believe me, Rosamunde, he's enraptured by you. I've told him what you're really like but he won't be deterred,' he teased. 'How about you?' he asked, stopping now to look out to sea. He looked all at once more serious. 'What do you think of him?'

'I like him,' she answered. Then, recognising that Ed might be just the man to take her mind off Benedict, she added, 'I really like him.'

Benedict turned to her, as if a little surprised. 'You do?'

'Yes,' replied Rosamunde. 'In fact, I don't suppose you could fix me up on a date with him, could you?' What harm could it do, after all, to go on just one date?

30.
JULY 1999

When Rosamunde told Stephen she'd broken off her engagement to Giles he breathed an enormous sigh of relief.

'And you?' she asked. 'Have you spoken to Jodie yet?'

'When I got back she'd left me a note saying she'd gone to visit her brother in Canterbury for ten days. He's not been well,' he explained. 'But as soon as she's back next Saturday I'll tell her. I can't tell her over the phone. It won't be long now,' he added. 'And in the meantime I'm free as a bird again. I managed to square some time off work. Shall I come and stay?'

Rosamunde had also managed to arrange some time off work and told Stephen he should but that they'd have to stay at the Vicarage, as Giles was in the process of moving his various possessions out of her flat. The prospect of Giles and Stephen meeting was too hideous to contemplate and she knew her father would welcome Stephen in spite of the difficult circumstances.

The first day was inevitably filled with stressful practicalities. Mrs Garfield, stalwart as ever, arrived at nine o'clock with a notepad and a list of phone numbers. They sat at the kitchen table with the telephone and took it in turns to call around while Stephen made endless cups of coffee for them and Bernie, less helpfully, looked at the crossword. The church arrangements were of course easy to untangle, but there was the reception to cancel, including the venue, food, drink and entertainment. Rosamunde was glad it wasn't her father having to stump up the bill – she and Giles had decided to pay for the wedding themselves and she'd now told Giles she would cover his half. It was the least she could do. Giles had tried to insist but Rosamunde wouldn't hear of it and thankfully she had a healthy-looking savings account.

There were also the guests to call and in a way this was worse, since they wanted explanations. After calling several of her own friends, Rosamunde was exhausted and Mrs Garfield was clearly uncomfortable with the task, so – by now almost in tears – Rosamunde made an SOS call to Kizzie, who'd kept a discreet distance since Rosamunde had told her the news, not wanting to intrude but making it clear she was at the end of a phone if needed. Kizzie left the girls with her mother and soon arrived at the Vicarage with kisses for everyone. She tucked her dark hair behind her pretty ears and quickly made her way down the list of friends and family like an efficient secretary at a multi-national company. Her direct yet gentle approach to those concerned made the task easier and by the end of the day everyone necessary had been notified. The little group – Bernie, Mrs Garfield, Kizzie, Stephen and Rosamunde – celebrated with an Indian takeaway.

Unscrambling a wedding at the last minute had not been pleasant, but there followed a magical week in which Bernie, Rosamunde and Stephen pottered around the Vicarage. Bernie had always liked Stephen and although he might well have disapproved of his conduct (and, indeed, of Rosamunde's) he managed to be delightfully un-judgemental. The three of them chattered easily away in the summer warmth of the pretty garden, which was full to bursting with burgeoning roses, and they took long walks along the cliffs. Bernie would often take himself off to give Rosamunde and Stephen time alone as well. Despite some lingering feelings of remorse over poor Giles (and, indeed, the unknown Jodie, whom Stephen telephoned every couple of days, re-appearing afterwards with his face etched with guilt), Rosamunde felt exquisitely happy.

It was as though the last twelve years had never happened and the couple had been plunged back to their youth, but with the benefit of experience and the knowledge that time was not to be squandered. The day before Stephen was to return to London they borrowed a boat from Gerard and ventured out to Kipper's Cove. The sea was a little choppy but it was sunny and the cove was sheltered. As soon as the boat was anchored the pair jumped off the deck into the icy depths of the ocean beneath them before surfacing with chattering teeth and racing each other to the shoreline. When they reached the shore they sprawled out on the sand to dry off, marvelling at having the whole beach to themselves.

'It's weird how you've barely aged,' remarked Stephen. 'Look at you. Still as slender as you always were.'

'I wasn't always slim,' Rosamunde reminded him. 'I went through a chubby stage when I was about thirteen or fourteen. I remember feeling terribly self-conscious.'

'I'd forgotten that,' chuckled Stephen. 'But you've always been beautiful.' He reached out and stroked Rosamunde's arm from shoulder to wrist. She turned to him.

'Was it the same?' she asked. 'When you met your wife? Did you have that feeling as though you were always meant to be together?'

They had skirted around the issue of relationships until now, but suddenly Rosamunde was overcome with curiosity. Stephen propped himself up on his elbows and looked pensively out to sea.

'I've never had that same connection with anyone,' he said. 'Not that I knew there was anything to compare things to until three years ago and then I put the feelings I remembered I'd had for you down to the intensity of youth. I've felt deeply for a few women over the years, especially Jodie. But there's never been quite that same passion or . . . well, affinity, I suppose you'd call it. Of course I had no idea what I was missing at the time and for the last three years I told myself if I ever saw you again I wouldn't feel a thing. How wrong I was,' he marvelled, shaking his head. 'And you?' he asked.

'Well, I pretty much shut up shop after I thought you'd died,' Rosamunde explained. 'I used to date the odd person while I was at university but nothing serious. It wasn't until I met Giles that I started to think I might be capable of another relationship after all. I was immediately taken with him,' she told Stephen honestly. 'He wasn't terribly attractive but he had this goodness about him. I was pretty much sold on him the very first day we met.'

'You're making me jealous.' Stephen grinned. 'I wish I hadn't asked.'

'It's worse for me!' Rosamunde laughed. 'You've been married for five years, for heaven's sake! I still can't believe it. What made you marry so young? You must have been, what, twenty-three?'

'I met Jodie soon after starting my first job at Ernst & Young. I'd had a couple of relationships at university but when I met her I was in a rushing phase of life. I wanted to climb the corporate ladder as quickly as possible. To get married and have children. I don't know why I wanted everything to happen so quickly. Perhaps it was the fear that my life had been spared once and I might not be so lucky the next time. I needed to live life quickly, fiercely. Jodie was working on reception at my office. It was just to earn some money – she's an actress, really.'

'An actress?' Rosamunde interrupted. Oh dear. So glamorous.

'Yes, she's still to have her lucky break but she's had bit parts on TV and worked in several large productions on the stage. Anyway, we started dating and we got on well. There were no thunderbolts but she was beautiful and we really loved each other. Actually, I still love her,' Stephen amended. 'The trouble is, I love you more.'

Rosamunde breathed a difficult breath and rolled onto her stomach, her face turned to Stephen. 'What does she look like?' she asked.

'Nothing like you,' Stephen told her. 'Funny, really. When my memories started to come back to me it surprised me that I'd gone for someone so different from you. She's very tall – my height. She has dark brown hair that she has cut into a bob, and hazel eyes. She's slim but sort of sturdier than you. She has a lovely smile.'

'Okay, stop there, Mister. You're killing me.'

'It's all right, Rosamunde. You don't need to worry. I love Jodie and she's beautiful but you and I are meant for each other, without question. I've no doubt in my mind.'

Rosamunde jumped up from the sand and put her hands out to pull Stephen up. 'Thank you,' she told him, simply, and, relieved, she raced down the sand into the shimmering sea again. 'Come on!' she shouted, and Stephen ran towards her, screeching at the cold and laughing, his dimples visible, his blond hair soaked.

'I love you, Stephen Jameson!' Rosamunde bellowed at him and he swam towards her, grabbing hold of her and squashing her cold, salty lips with his own.

'I love you too, babe,' he told her. 'More than anything.'

31.
WEDNESDAY 17TH DECEMBER 2014

Rosamunde woke up with a banging headache and that feeling of dread that inevitably accompanies a hangover.

'Oh dear,' she grumbled to herself as she tried to recall the events of the night before. They were a little hazy in parts. There was a knock at the door.

'Come in,' she croaked.

'Morning, Rosamunde,' chirped Mrs Garfield. 'Beautiful day out there. Crisp as you like. Here, I've brought you a cuppa. Bernie's just gone across to the church hall to help get it ready for Saturday's Christmas market. He said you were out late. Thought you might like a good brew,' she said as she placed the steaming mug on Rosamunde's bedside table and drew back the curtains.

Rosamunde's eyes protested at the glittering morning sunshine but she heaved herself out of bed to look out of the window, and even in her washed-out state she was able to appreciate the beauty of the day. There was a frost on the last of the autumn leaves, making them sparkle like precious jewels.

'Thank you,' she managed, flopping back down into bed again.

'Heavy night?' asked Mrs Garfield with a knowing look. 'I remember hangovers like that from my younger days,' she added. 'There was one night,' she told Rosamunde, confidentially, 'when I was that drunk Mr Garfield had to carry me home from the pub. When I got back I was sick all over the clean laundry. Had to wash it all again.' Rosamunde smiled weakly.

'I'll leave you to it,' Mrs Garfield told her and she was out just as swiftly as she'd bustled in.

The date had started well enough. Ed had arrived at the Vicarage and chatted affably to Bernie whilst Rosamunde abided by Coco Chanel's rule of taking off one accessory before she descended the narrow staircase. She was greeted by her date, who'd complimented her on her outfit, an emerald-green jumper dress with thick tights and chestnut boots, with her mother's old pearl earrings and a gold bracelet, but no necklace – the accessory she'd forsaken. Rosamunde had used some of the make-up Rachel had persuaded her to buy in London and she felt good, if a little nervous. It had been some time since she'd last gone on a date.

Ed was quick to put her at ease, politely holding out her coat for her and then the door of his old MG.

'I thought we'd go into Thatchley,' he said. 'Benedict told me about a nice Italian there – La Barca?'

'My favourite,' replied Rosamunde as she snuggled into her faux-fur coat. Good old Benedict. He knew how she loved that restaurant. She adored Italian food.

The restaurant was warm and inviting and the Italian waiters fussed around Rosamunde with kisses, taking her coat and leading the couple to a corner table near the window. The lights were dim, candles had been lit and a festive atmosphere filled the bistro. It couldn't have been a better venue for a first date and Rosamunde found Ed an easy companion, full of thrilling stories and interested in her without being too probing.

'Benedict tells me you're a lawyer,' he said as they tucked into salty calamari.

'Was,' explained Rosamunde. 'I haven't worked in a law firm for fifteen years, although I suppose technically I'm still a lawyer.'

'So what have the last fifteen years entailed?' he asked. Rosamunde could tell he was genuinely interested from his alert blue eyes and steady gaze. And all at once he reminded her of someone. Taken aback, she found herself gulping down a large slurp of wine. She hadn't noticed the similarity until now but there was a confidence in his manner and a twinkle in his eyes that was exactly like Stephen. All of a sudden Rosamunde knew she had to get away from the table. She excused herself and rushed upstairs to the ladies where she splashed her face with cool water, giving herself a stern telling off – it was crazy to be so affected by the memory of Stephen after all these years. She thought about him now, picturing his face, and bit her lip. But then she smiled. It had been a shock to be so suddenly reminded of Stephen by Ed, but she realised now that she could look back peacefully. She returned, better composed, to a rather bemused-looking Ed.

'Sorry about that,' she said.

'Not at all. I hope it wasn't something you ate? Or, worse, something I said?'

'Oh gosh, no – neither,' Rosamunde replied and she proceeded to tell him about the last fifteen years. How she'd started her travels in France before heading to more exotic destinations – India, then Cambodia, Thailand, Singapore, Borneo, Indonesia and finally Australia.

'Were you working?'

'Sometimes. I worked as a volunteer at orphanages in India and Cambodia, which was heartbreaking and wonderful all at the same time. Then I conducted myself like an eighteen-year-old in Thailand before calming down again and getting jobs in wildlife parks all over the show. I worked at an orang-utan rehabilitation centre in Borneo and ended up with a job in Australia working with koalas. I really felt I'd found my vocation. I also managed to get some quite lucrative work at a mining company in Perth, but it was working with animals that I really loved.'

Ed, as a vet, was interested in the work Rosamunde had been involved in at wildlife centres, and the evening was soon back on an even keel.

They ate spaghetti and then shared a scrumptious homemade tiramisu, which was presented to them with a sparkler on top even though it was neither of their birthdays. By the time their coffee arrived Rosamunde was feeling rather drunk. Ed was driving so she'd enjoyed the lion's share of the wine. She downed her coffee but it did little to sober her up and she found herself feeling a little unsteady on her feet.

'What shall we do now?' asked Ed as they made their way into the arctic night air. 'It's only half ten. Fancy a quick drink back at The Dragon's Head?'

Ed had been abstemious but he was keen to catch up with Rosamunde and so as soon as they entered the warmth of the pub he ordered some shots as well as long drinks for them both.

It had been many years since Rosamunde had downed shots and she'd forgotten how much fun it could be. By the time the pub closed Rosamunde was sure she was making little sense but Ed didn't seem to mind. He'd walked her up the hill to the Vicarage and, at this point, Rosamunde's memories became a little foggy.

Rosamunde eventually clambered out of bed and padded to the bathroom where she ran a bath and poured in some oil scented with eucalyptus, which she hoped would help her head. As she lay back in the steaming, scented water she tried to remember the end of the evening before to no avail. It wasn't until she was sitting at the kitchen table with a large mug of coffee that she recalled the kiss. She hadn't invited Ed in but they'd enjoyed a very lengthy kiss on the doorstep, like teenagers. At the memory Rosamunde found her hangover becoming decidedly worse. There had been nothing wrong with the kiss – in fact, it had been quite nice. But she knew she wasn't interested in Ed, perfect though he was; she wished she were. The reality was she was in love with Benedict – it was crystal clear to her now, no matter how futile it was. Rosamunde was staggered at how quickly she'd managed to get herself into a romantic mess considering she was now the grand old age of forty-four and only a few days ago had been more than content to be single for the rest of her days.

She would have liked to hide away all day but she'd promised Ed last night she'd help him decorate Benedict's cottage for Christmas while he was taking Humphrey for a mid-morning walk – that she *did* remember: Benedict never bothered with Christmas decorations and both she and Ed thought that was rather 'bah, humbug' of him. She'd assured Ed (several times) that she'd be there at eleven o'clock and it was now a quarter to, so she brushed her teeth for the third time and found her coat. *Here goes*, she thought to herself as she drove Bernie's car the short distance to Benedict's cottage.

She knocked on the door with trepidation but was relieved to find that Ed didn't draw her into a clinch. Instead, he briefly dropped a kiss on her cheek before offering her a coffee and leading the way to the sitting room where he'd just erected a Christmas tree. Thankfully there was no talk of the evening before and they bustled about decorating the tree with tinsel and some baubles Rosamunde had brought with her that hadn't been used at the Vicarage. Ed had bought some Christmas lights and had also been out and about collecting holly and ivy, which they now balanced on picture frames and between beams. As a final touch, Ed produced some mistletoe, which he fixed to one of the beams with a drawing pin.

'There!' he announced, smiling his crinkly-eyed smile at Rosamunde. 'Now come here, you,' he said pulling her firmly into his arms and kissing her with an unmistakably intense passion. Again, there was nothing wrong with the kiss – it was actually quite wonderful – but Rosamunde knew she was getting herself into deep water.

'I take it last night was a success, then!' exclaimed Benedict as he entered the room to find his friend and Rosamunde entwined. Rosamunde, who had jumped back from Ed like a scalded cat, hurriedly showed Benedict the details of their festive handiwork. Ed said he would make more coffee and pottered off to the kitchen.

'You really do like him, then?' asked Benedict as he put a match to the fire to make the sitting room even more festive.

'I like him, yes, but not like that,' Rosamunde whispered.

'Well, call me old-fashioned but I suspect Ed may be thinking otherwise right now,' replied Benedict with a raised eyebrow.

'It's complicated.'

'It always was with you,' Benedict remarked, without his usual teasing humour. He turned away from her. It occurred to her then that perhaps Benedict had feelings for Ed that were more than just platonic, in the same way she did for him. She also felt hurt. She'd always put her disastrous love life down to bad luck but perhaps it *was* just her? It certainly seemed she was incapable of enjoying a simple life free of relationship concerns. Why – when she was perfectly happy single – did she have to fall in love with a gay man and lead his perfect-for-her best friend up the garden path, all in the space of a few short days?

'I have to go,' she said and before anyone could persuade her otherwise she grabbed her coat and keys and left. She arrived home and promptly burst into tears.

Mrs Garfield returned to the Vicarage for her afternoon stint of cleaning to find Rosamunde blowing her nose. In typical Mrs Garfield fashion she was quick to comfort and dole out more tissues but she wouldn't allow Rosamunde to languish.

'I'm baking mince pies before I set about my cleaning, so you come through to the kitchen with me and get started on the pastry,' she ordered. 'There's nothing as therapeutic as baking and you can tell me all about this mess you've got yourself into.' She didn't add 'this time' but Rosamunde wondered if she, too, thought Rosamunde was more than a little disaster prone.

The two of them were soon ensconced in the homely task of weighing out ingredients and by the time the mince pies were in the Aga Mrs Garfield had listened to Rosamunde's plight. She was silent for a moment and then she turned to Rosamunde, placed her hands on her shoulders and looked into her eyes.

'I'll tell you what you must do, Rosamunde, though I think you know this yourself. You must go and see Ed this evening and tell him the truth. You have to be brave.'

Rosamunde nodded and sank into Mrs Garfield's embrace. 'Thank you,' she told her. 'I don't know what I'd do without you.'

'Get away with you!' Mrs Garfield replied, swatting Rosamunde with a tea towel, then yelping as she realised the mince pies had been in the Aga for too long and would soon burn to a crisp.

At six o'clock Rosamunde rang Ed and arranged to meet him in a quiet corner of The Dragon's Head.

∽

'What's all this about, then?' asked Ed. 'Not that I'm not pleased to see you,' he added, with his wide, confident smile. Rosamunde took a deep breath and started to explain that she didn't want to string him along any more than she had already; that she liked him very much but that she was in love with someone else. Ed's pride must have been a little dented but he was very gentlemanly. He looked at her ruefully.

'Don't tell me,' he said. 'You're in love with Benedict?' Rosamunde was taken aback. Her silence said it all.

'Story of my life recently,' Ed shrugged. 'The number of women I've met since my divorce who've ended up falling for Benedict when he's been staying with me.' Rosamunde felt dreadful.

'I'm sorry,' she said. 'I'm sorry for us ridiculous women, too, falling for someone who's gay.'

Ed looked up, his piercing eyes confused.

'But, Rosamunde,' he said. 'Benedict's not gay.'

32.
JULY 1999

Rosamunde spent what should have been her wedding day on tenterhooks as she counted down the hours until she would see Stephen again – until, finally, the two of them would be at liberty to start all over again as a couple. She knew it was too soon for such thoughts but she found herself daydreaming about a house in the country, dogs and children.

Stephen had left the night before and Jodie was due to arrive back at their house in Putney this morning. It had been agreed that Stephen would immediately explain everything to Jodie before meeting Rosamunde at Paddington station at three o'clock. From there they planned to have a half restoring, half celebratory afternoon tea at a plush London hotel before returning to Potter's Cove.

This meant that Rosamunde needed to leave the Vicarage mid-morning. She dressed with care – a summery cream halter-neck dress, delicate tan sandals and a pale green cashmere cardigan in case it should cloud over. She had a small satchel she wore across her body (she'd never been a huge fan of handbags). Her dark red hair was freshly washed and dried and the bright sun brought out its natural coppery highlights. She had on a little make-up – some powder, mascara and pink lip gloss to enhance her full lips.

During the long journey Rosamunde found her heart fluttering with nerves. She felt like a sixteen-year-old about to meet her first date rather than a grown woman of twenty-eight. Finally, she arrived at Paddington station. It was a quarter to three. She spotted a small newsagent's on the platform where she was due to meet Stephen and decided to buy a magazine. It was a bit pointless, since she would hardly be able to concentrate on it, but it took a few minutes to select *Marie Claire*, hand over a note, wait for the change and finally flick through the pages as she sat on a bench and watched the platform clock. She wished they'd agreed that Stephen should simply telephone her rather than meeting at the station in this old-fashioned way, but he'd explained it would be difficult to call her from home and Rosamunde didn't have a mobile so they'd had to set a place.

As the clock hands reached three Rosamunde's heart was in her throat as she began to panic that he had changed his mind. Perhaps Jodie had begged him to stay and he'd caved in, or, worse, decided he loved her more than Rosamunde after all. But then, suddenly, she saw him rushing down the platform steps and she felt quite lightheaded with relief. He was here and she'd been a fool to doubt him for a second.

'Rosamunde!' Stephen exclaimed as he grabbed her to him and they embraced, quite unaware of the curious glances they were receiving from passers-by. He pulled away from her and as she looked up at him she saw tears pouring from his turquoise eyes.

'What's wrong?' she asked. 'Why tears?' She rubbed them with her hands. 'It's okay,' she reassured him. 'It's done now.'

Stephen gulped, his face all crumpled. 'But it's not,' he said. 'Rosamunde, Jodie's pregnant. She just told me. We're having a baby. I'm sorry, babe. I'm so sorry. But I can't leave her now. I simply can't.'

As the words sank in, time seemed to stand still. Rosamunde thought it quite strange that the shattering of her heart wasn't audible.

33.
SATURDAY 20TH DECEMBER 2014

Rosamunde was no longer happily single – such a state of affairs was only possible when you weren't suffering from unrequited love. Her emotions ran from elated – Benedict wasn't gay so perhaps he might have feelings for her too? – to hopeless. After all, he'd made no attempts to disillusion her about the fact that she (and everyone else) thought he was gay, and he hadn't made a single gesture or comment that she could construe as remotely romantic.

But there was little time to dwell, for early on this icy Saturday morning the Vicarage had been invaded by Rachel and her family, who'd left London at five o'clock to avoid the pre-Christmas traffic and arrive before the snow that was forecast to fall in the afternoon. Rachel had emerged from the car in a cloud of Chanel No. 5, wrapped in a deep red belted winter coat that matched her lips. She looked like a film star, not a mother of two arrived in Potter's Cove for a family Christmas.

It was now ten o'clock and Simon had taken two very excited bundled-up children down to the beach to allow Rosamunde and Rachel time to finalise plans for the party. Bernie was at the church hall where he was closeted away in a makeshift grotto playing the part of Father Christmas at the annual Christmas market.

Once satisfied everything had been thought of for the party, Rachel, nibbling on a mince pie, took a good look at her sister.

'Are you okay?' she asked. 'You're looking very pale.'

'Fine,' Rosamunde replied. She didn't want to get into her relationship troubles with Rachel right now. 'Come on,' she said, scraping back the pine kitchen chair and grabbing her coat. 'Let's find Simon and the kids and head over to the market. Do you think Lily will suss on that Father Christmas is her grandfather?'

'I do hope not. That *would* be embarrassing! Imagine if my daughter was responsible for revealing the myth of Father Christmas to all the children of Potter's Cove!' hooted Rachel.

The market was alive with activity as all the villagers began to embrace the Christmas period. The large – usually freezing – hall was warm and bright, with a festive scent of pine emanating from a large tree in the corner, and there were trestle tables set up as stalls in a rectangular shape. Immediately on the left was the bottle stall where Simon had been tempted to stop, whereupon he immediately won a bottle of Dom Perignon. With such success under his belt he decided to loiter a little longer, so the female party moved on to scrutinise the other stalls with the children in tow. There was a stall selling homemade teddy bears, which grabbed Lily's and Art's attention. Rachel – who spoiled the children dreadfully – immediately caved in and bought them a bear each.

The next table showcased delicious-looking homemade cakes and buns and alongside that was the tombola, which enthralled the children as they spun the brightly coloured wooden barrel and selected tickets from within the cavity. Rosamunde managed to win a selection pack of chocolate, which she donated to her niece and nephew. There was a stall selling beautiful African jewellery (Rosamunde bought a striking silver bangle for Kizzie) and a sweet old lady who'd lived in the village all her life – genuinely called Lavender Hanky – was, appropriately, selling embroidered handkerchiefs. Neither Rosamunde nor Rachel used hankies but they couldn't bear to disappoint dear Lavender so they stocked up.

There was a second-hand book seller that magnetised Rosamunde but there were other stalls that couldn't tempt the women – a lascivious man they remembered of old was selling bric-à-brac and they steered well clear of him. As they pottered around, the sisters found themselves endlessly bumping into familiar old faces and exchanging small talk, though they both managed to avoid Clara, who was showing off her husband and baby as though she'd just won them in the raffle.

When Lily and Art began to drive them mad with their begging they took the children through to the grotto where they each sat on one of Father Christmas's knees. A local reporter was at the market and he took a photograph of the scene, which would later appear in the *Gazette* with the caption: 'Little Art and Lily had no idea that Father Christmas was actually their grandfather – the Reverend Bernie Pemberton of Potter's Cove'.

The man with the long white beard asked the children what they'd like for Christmas and Lily told him in some detail the items on her list and where Father Christmas would be able to buy them. She was a very practical girl and wasn't going to take any chances. They left satisfied customers, each with a small gift from Santa's sack to tide them over until Christmas Day.

By lunchtime, feeling quite exhausted, the sisters, Simon and the children were about to head to the pub for some food when they bumped into Benedict and Ed at, predictably, the bottle stall. Rosamunde made the introductions and asked if they'd won anything.

'Not a sausage,' Ed replied, grinning broadly. Rosamunde was glad he didn't seem to be holding her recent revelation against her.

'We're off to the pub for lunch now,' Rosamunde told them. 'Would you like to join us?' She willed Benedict to say yes. He looked at her.

'Why not?' he replied.

They strolled across from the church hall to the pub – a large and merry gang. The children were enthralled by Humphrey – Art kept trying to ride him as though he were a horse, and Humphrey was obligingly long-suffering about this. Rachel and Rosamunde hung back slightly.

'Bloody hell, Rosamunde, he's gorgeous!' declared Rachel, lighting up a cigarette.

'Who?' Rosamunde desperately hoped it wasn't Benedict who'd caught her sister's fancy. She couldn't bear the thought of any further competition.

'The guy with Benedict, of course. What's his name again?'

'Ed,' Rosamunde replied. 'But haven't you got enough on your plate with Simon and the Spanish guy?'

'I'm not saying I'm going to devour him,' replied Rachel. 'A girl's allowed to look, after all.'

Yes, thought Rosamunde, as she observed Benedict with the children, his head tipped back in abandoned laughter at one of Lily's remarks. *A girl's allowed to look.*

During lunch Rosamunde and Benedict sat next to each other around the large oak table the group had commandeered and she revelled in the fact they were able to chat and fool around as they had before Ed had arrived in the village. There was one subject of conversation she was desperate to bring up, namely why on earth Benedict had pretended for the last three years to be gay. Ed had clammed up on the subject when asked, insisting that Rosamunde should speak to Benedict about it herself. But she recognised it wasn't the right time.

However, as luck would have it, an opportunity presented itself later in the day. The lunch had turned out to be rather liquid and Rachel suggested everyone troop back to the Vicarage for tea and mince pies. They had just rehydrated and further filled themselves with food by the log fire when Art spotted something.

''no, 'no, 'no!' he chanted. No one understood what he meant apart from his older sister. She looked out of the window.

'Yes, Arty! Snow!' she interpreted. Everyone was suddenly alive with excitement and soon the party was wrapping themselves up in coats and scarves and rushing outside to lark around in the thick snowflakes that were falling heavily from the dark sky. As if by unspoken agreement Rosamunde and Benedict held back, remaining by the fire with Humphrey (for such an athletic dog he was surprisingly idle) and helping themselves to more tea from the pot.

'I hear you've found out my little secret,' said Benedict. He'd decided to be direct and Rosamunde was grateful. This was a conversation they needed to have whilst they had the room to themselves.

'Ed told me,' Rosamunde admitted, trusting that Ed hadn't divulged her own little secret to Benedict. 'I'm confused,' she added. Benedict sighed.

'I should have explained before,' he said, looking suitably contrite. 'You remember we had that chat in Thatchley in the graveyard? About Clara?' he asked. Rosamunde nodded.

'Well, there was a part of the story I didn't explain. You know how Clara reacted when I tried to end the relationship the first time? Well, I was absolutely desperate to find a reason to finish with her that would end things once and for all. Then one day, suddenly, it occurred to me that if I told her I was gay she would have to move on. It was risky, of course. I didn't want to provoke another overdose. But eventually I did it and it worked beautifully. I think Clara felt better for knowing it wasn't her that was the issue, if you can call it that, but me.'

Benedict rubbed at the knots in his broad shoulders.

'But I didn't want there to be any risk she'd find out I'd lied to her so I decided to spin the same yarn to everyone – my family and friends. The only person I didn't bother pretending to was Ed as he wasn't in the area and didn't know anyone round here. It's only in the last year he's been to stay a few times – I usually visit him. And I needed at least one person I could be completely normal with. As time went by and Clara found a new man, I could of course have easily confessed my tall story to everyone, but by then I'd discovered the benefits of being gay.' Benedict grinned ruefully.

'Such as?' asked Rosamunde.

'Better relationships with my female family members and friends; not being continually set up with supposedly eligible single women I couldn't have been less interested in after my disastrous relationship with Clara. So I kept up the pretence. And then, of course, you returned to Potter's Cove and I couldn't possibly tell you the truth when my own sister didn't know it. I never actually lied to you, though. You just made assumptions and I didn't disabuse you. I hope you don't feel I've betrayed you.' Benedict's large dark eyes met Rosamunde's and she felt herself softening. She could understand his reasons, however misguided.

'But are you sure you're not gay?' asked Rosamunde. 'Because I was utterly convinced. I mean, for a start, you like shopping!'

'Don't be ridiculous,' Benedict replied, a smile playing on his lips. 'I can't stand it, actually. I do most of my Christmas shopping in November to get the wretched task out of the way, but you seemed to like it so much on our trips to Thatchley and I was happy to play along. And anyway, I'm sure there are some straight men who like shopping and some gay men who hate it. You mustn't be so sweeping in your generalisations,' he teased.

'So have you had any relationships since you started this pretence?' asked Rosamunde. 'It can't have been easy.' Benedict shook his head.

'Clara put me off relationships for life, to be honest,' he said. 'I'm quite happy to be on my own. That's why the pretence was so convenient. But listen, you won't tell Kizzie yet, will you? I'll explain everything to her – and my parents – when I find the right moment.'

'Of course I won't,' replied Rosamunde, and before their discussion could continue further, they heard the over-excited chatter of the rest of the group returning to the warmth of the cottage. Benedict got up and reached over to Rosamunde. He landed a kiss on her forehead.

'Thank you,' he said. If Rosamunde had been twenty-five years younger she'd have resolved never to wash her forehead again. As it was, she took a deep breath and smiled. He'd now told her the truth, but there was a part of it she hadn't wanted to hear. *'Clara put me off relationships for life,'* he'd said. *'I'm quite happy to be on my own.'* Rosamunde had known those sentiments herself, but now things had changed. Suddenly she felt she couldn't be in the same room as Benedict a moment longer and, in order to escape, announced she was going upstairs to wrap presents.

When she'd closed the wooden door of her bedroom Rosamunde sat on the edge of the bed and looked at herself in the dressing table mirror. She looked frazzled. She had to get her head around the situation and quickly. She needed to accept the fact that, although Benedict wasn't gay after all, he had no interest in her. She should just enjoy their friendship. *Rosamunde,* she said to herself silently, *you have to get over this. Be happy alone. Be content with Benedict as a friend.* She sat still for a moment until she heard the taps of the bath being turned on next door. Rachel must be bathing the children. She took a deep breath. Then she found her gifts, some wrapping paper, scissors and Sellotape. It was time to wrap.

34.
AUGUST 1999

When she looked back at the aftermath of that fateful day in July she supposed she'd had a minor breakdown. Initially she was strangely calm and accepting. It was as if, in her deepest subconscious, she'd known Stephen would never really be hers but she'd so much enjoyed the possibility that he might be. Now reality had come crashing down, quashing all her hopes and dreams.

She made the journey home, alone, where she told her father the situation.

'Will you go back to Giles?' he asked, then – seeing her face – added quickly, 'No, of course not. Silly question.'

Days passed. She didn't cry. She was frozen in a strange paralysis that seemed to be preventing any facial expression, action or movement.

Eventually she agreed to see Kizzie, who'd been trying to come round since she'd heard the news from Bernie. It was the trigger Rosamunde feared it would be and the floodgates were opened to tears, anger and despair. She began to develop an irrational fear of stepping outside the Vicarage or of seeing anyone. The only solace she found was at the bottom of a bottle of wine and when Bernie began to find an unusually large number of bottles by the bin he tried to break through Rosamunde's defensive wall and talk to her. But his words and suggestions had little effect. The only advice she took was to ring her employers to explain her absence and take the month's leave she'd planned to use for her honeymoon.

A month after the Saturday of Stephen's news Rosamunde found herself looking out of her bedroom window at the village below. It was a busy, sunny day in Potter's Cove and she didn't want to venture out, but she'd drunk the Vicarage dry and desperately needed to buy some wine from the local shop. She went to the bathroom and looked at herself in the mirror above the sink. She looked like someone she didn't recognise: gaunt, pale, her hair lank, enormous bags under her eyes, which no longer glittered with life but instead looked as though the light in them had been extinguished. She splashed her face with water, cleaned her teeth and dressed in the nearest pair of jeans and t-shirt she could find. Her father was nowhere to be found so she crept out of the back door, leaving it unlocked as they tended to.

She was about to enter the shop when she spotted Benedict coming out with newspapers and a pint of milk. He must be home visiting his family. She wondered if Clara was with him. Rosamunde didn't want to see either of them so she quickly walked by until she found herself suddenly at the path leading up to the church. As she stood there, looking up at the imposing building, the clock struck three. She looked back at the shop and saw Benedict had stopped just outside it, chatting to a friend he'd bumped into. She decided to take refuge just for a moment in the porch of the church but, once there, she found herself drawn in.

Despite – or perhaps because of – being a vicar's daughter, Rosamunde had never been a deeply religious person but she'd always enjoyed the rituals of a Sunday service and the soothing, peaceful comfort a church could provide. She pushed the heavy oak door open and poked her head around to check there were no helpful flower arrangers or even her father inside. She found it empty and cool. Rosamunde walked tentatively towards the altar and perched on a pew at the front of the church.

She looked up at the enormous stained glass window above the altar and as she did so a strange thing happened. She felt herself going into a sort of trance and then, all of a sudden, there was a pressure on her head. It reminded her of the sensation she'd experienced when, at the age of twelve, she'd been confirmed. The bishop had blessed her and pressed down on her head as he did so. Right now it was that same feeling – a heaviness bearing down on her scalp and a soporific sensation reminiscent of that moment in Harrods when she felt her mother's presence with her. But this wasn't her mother. Rosamunde wasn't sure what this was, but she was certain there was a greater power to this feeling. Eventually, when she began to feel more normal again, she got up, with heavy legs, and found herself dropping to the tiled floor of the aisle, just in front of the altar. She allowed her forehead to rest on the cool tiles and as she did so a loud sob shot out of her mouth. But there were no tears. She emerged from the church, blinking at the strong sunlight, feeling shaken and yet strangely stronger. She must have been in there for less than half an hour but the experience felt momentous.

When she arrived back at the Vicarage, having forgotten entirely about going to the shop, she saw a blue Fiesta outside. Inside, at the kitchen table, was Granny Dupont. She didn't waste any time. As soon as Rosamunde entered the sunny kitchen she got straight to the point.

'I think you need to get away, dear,' she said. 'I have a nephew in France – Pierre Lacroix. He and his wife would be happy to have you to stay.'

Granny Dupont had a knack, Rosamunde decided, for arriving at the critical moment. The very next day, after handing in her notice at work (and wangling an almost immediate departure),

Rosamunde booked herself a flight, and a few days later she arrived in the late summer heat of the Dordogne. She'd left Potter's Cove with a large suitcase after a tearful embrace with her father, who'd sweetly agreed to arrange for Rosamunde's flat to be let. She had no idea when she'd return but for now Granny Dupont had been right – she needed to get away.

And France, she decided, was as good a place as anywhere to start her journey.

PART THREE

PART THREE

35.
TUESDAY 23RD DECEMBER 2014

The 23rd December was, of course, one of the most wonderful days of Christmas – full of excitement and bustle. Rosamunde awoke feeling quite bright. She'd successfully parcelled away her yearnings for Benedict and was gradually coming to accept the idea of remaining on her own again. She'd wrapped all her presents and the Vicarage was full of life and festivities. She was sitting at the kitchen table helping herself to breakfast while Lily told her about the various problems associated with having a younger brother and how it was such a shame her mother hadn't managed to provide her with a sister. Poor Art sat there as good as gold listening to his sister's complaints. As she listened to her young niece she felt full of anticipation for the days of Christmas ahead.

Then the telephone rang. It was Kizzie, in floods of tears.

'What's wrong?' asked Rosamunde, immediately full of concern, but her friend was unintelligible. In the end she told her to sit tight and that she'd be right round. Rosamunde quickly squared it with her father that she could take his car, grabbed her coat and headed out to find thick snow on the ground. It was clear she wasn't going to get anywhere in the Citroën. There was only one thing to do. She retrieved her mobile phone from her bag.

'I need to ask you a favour,' she said a moment later.

Benedict immediately dropped everything and was at the Vicarage within ten minutes in his Land Rover.

'What on earth can be wrong?' he asked Rosamunde. She was torn. She didn't want to betray Kizzie's confidence (it was clear Benedict had no idea about his sister's suspicions) but she equally didn't want Benedict to worry unduly.

'I'm sorry, Benedict, but I can't say. It's nothing life threatening,' she assured him. 'I'll explain to Kizzie that you're outside and she may well suggest you come in. Are you happy to wait until I give you the go-ahead?' she asked.

'Of course. I'll take Humphrey for a walk around the estate. She obviously needs you. Call me on my mobile.'

When Rosamunde rang on the bell she was astonished to find Gerard opening the front door. She'd rather expected he would have been hoofed out by now.

'You look surprised to see me,' he remarked. 'Kizzie's in a bit of a state, I'm afraid. She's up in her bedroom. See what you can do?' he asked, his eyes pleading. Despite herself, Rosamunde felt a little bit of sympathy for him.

Rosamunde found Kizzie under the duvet. She poked her head out when she heard the bedroom door open and her usually pretty face was a swollen red mess.

'It's true, then?' Rosamunde asked. 'He's having an affair?' This prompted Kizzie to burst into a flood of tears.

'I almost wish he was,' she said. 'Rosamunde, he's got cancer. He was never having an affair. He was going to appointments at the hospital in Totnes. He's ill, Rosamunde. He might die!'

Rosamunde felt her legs go quite weak. So it *had* been Gerard she'd seen in Totnes the other day after all. She plonked herself heavily on the side of the bed and wrapped Kizzie into a bear hug, trying to soothe her friend.

'And now I'm the one freaking out and that makes it worse,' sobbed Kizzie. 'I should be supporting him, not collapsing in a heap.'

'Give it time,' said Rosamunde. 'It's the shock. Gerard's had time to take it all in. You've only just found out.'

Eventually, Kizzie calmed down. Rosamunde ran her a bath, pouring in some calming lavender bath oil, and took her friend through to the bathroom like an invalid. She undressed her and got her into the bath, then waited quietly whilst Kizzie lay still in the deep water, the only noise an occasional shudder left over from her sobbing. Once she'd helped dress her friend she led her downstairs.

'We need to find out all the facts,' Rosamunde said. Downstairs, a forlorn-looking Gerard was feeding Emma at the kitchen table. Rosamunde took over so he could concentrate on explaining everything properly to Kizzie, who had gone into meltdown as soon as she heard the word 'cancer' earlier that morning.

It was extremely worrying, of course, but it transpired the cancer – prostate cancer – had been caught at an early stage and that Gerard would be able to have the tumour removed in an operation, followed by a short stint of radiotherapy. There was an excellent chance he would be back to good health in a matter of months.

It was about an hour and a half into her visit that Rosamunde suddenly remembered Benedict. Poor Benedict – so discreet and who must by now have been absolutely freezing. She dashed out of the front door and found him huddled up in the Land Rover with Humphrey.

'I'm so sorry,' she said. 'You'd better come in.'

Explanations were made to him and then Rosamunde decided to make herself useful and prepare some lunch. Benedict went round to the neighbours' to pick up Harriet, who'd been dispatched there by Gerard before his revelation this morning. She managed to lighten the atmosphere very swiftly.

Nonetheless, it had been a very emotional morning and by the afternoon, when Rosamunde and Benedict decided it was time to leave the family to it (the older girls had been away overnight and now needed to be told the difficult news), the pair were feeling jangled. They drove in silence until Benedict turned the radio on briefly, but the jolly tune of *The Most Wonderful Time of the Year* didn't match their moods and he turned it quickly off again.

'I feel we should cancel the party,' Rosamunde said eventually.

'No, you mustn't,' Benedict replied, sensibly. 'You heard Gerard – he wants to carry on as normal. He'd hate it if we cancelled.'

'I know,' Rosamunde sighed. 'But who feels like celebrating?'

'Tomorrow's another day,' said Benedict. 'We'll buoy ourselves up by then. Here we are,' he said, turning into the Vicarage drive.

'Thank you,' Rosamunde told him and kissed him goodbye.

Inside Rosamunde was amazed to find that the atmosphere was just as festive as when she'd left this morning even though the world had turned on its axis as far as she was concerned. She hated to be the harbinger of doom but she explained everything briefly to Bernie and her sister then retreated to her bedroom for some peace and quiet. She resolved to perk herself up later but for now she felt shocked and devastated for her best friend and her family.

At teatime there was a knock on the door. It was Bernie.

'I'm exhausted,' Rosamunde told him as she looked up from her bed.

'It's the shock,' he replied, handing her a cup of tea. 'I know it's a terrible piece of news but it sounds to me as though all will be well. It's useful to have faith, you know, Rosie. Not just because it's a comfort to ourselves, but because it's an enormous help to the person who's ill.'

'You're right,' Rosamunde smiled weakly at her father. 'It's so easy to imagine the worst. Much harder to have faith that it will work out all right.'

'Come on,' Bernie said, pulling Rosamunde up off the bed. 'Come and have high tea with us all.'

Feeling mildly guilty for returning to the festivities, Rosamunde joined in the tea, which was a comforting mix of crustless sandwiches and scones with jam and Devon cream. Then, later in the afternoon, she shook off any lingering feelings of guilt and sadness so that she could be businesslike about party preparations.

Benedict and her father were right – the party must go on.

36.
AUGUST 1999
FRANCE

It was seven in the evening and still bright as noontime. Rosamunde had unpacked and showered and she made her way downstairs out onto the terrace, where she found Pierre and Cecile enjoying an aperitif.

'Come and join us,' Pierre said as soon as he spotted Rosamunde. She'd been amazed at how fluent his English was when he met her at the airport earlier in the day, though Cecile couldn't speak much at all. It transpired Pierre had been sent to an English boarding school, hence his almost accent-less English, which put Rosamunde to shame as she spoke very little French despite her heritage.

Rosamunde sat down at the wooden table, which was as rustic as the rest of the villa. It was all very grand in scale – the house would cost a fortune in England – but there was an absolute simplicity to it in terms of décor and ambience. *Rustic* was the word. However, Rosamunde had been pleased to spot the luxury of a swimming pool beside the terrace.

'You've unpacked? You're feeling at home?' asked Pierre as he handed Rosamunde a glass of champagne, which was delicious and immediately began to relax her. When she'd arrived at the airport earlier she'd suddenly found herself wondering what on earth she was doing, coming here with no plan whatsoever as the guest of two unwitting hosts who probably had no idea why this young woman had been foisted upon them. But they were certainly kindly and welcoming so far.

'Yes, I'm all unpacked thank you, Pierre,' she replied, closing her eyes and feeling the warmth of the sunshine on her eyelids.

'You're tired?' he asked, endlessly solicitous.

'No, relaxed,' smiled Rosamunde, opening her eyes again and squinting into the sun. She'd forgotten sunglasses – she would need to buy some.

'Your grandmother said you'd had a difficult time recently,' Pierre said. 'I don't wish to pry but I suspect it was a love affair?' he asked.

Rosamunde looked at him. Everything about Pierre was round – large, round eyes as dark as treacle, a ruddy round face, a large round belly. Cecile was almost exactly the same but with long dark hair that had started to grey, which she plaited in a twist so that the plait rested over the front of her right shoulder. Despite Cecile's lack of English, she seemed to have grasped the expression 'love affair', as her interest had perked up. She looked at Rosamunde inquisitively.

'Yes, it's a long story, I'm afraid,' Rosamunde said. 'How long have you got?'

'We have all evening,' said Pierre, and so Rosamunde began to explain all about Stephen and Giles and the cancelled wedding and Jodie's pregnancy. She felt it only fair to explain the whole story to the couple since they had been kind enough to put her up and were obviously interested to know what had led her to them.

Here and there Pierre translated for Cecile, who would gasp and shake her head. Eventually, the story told, the woman heaved herself up from her chair and planted two fierce kisses on Rosamunde's cheeks before wiping tears away from her large dark eyes. Rosamunde was touched. She also felt lighter – as if by telling the story she had lifted a part of the weight of it from her body.

'Now we eat,' said Cecile, and she bustled off to prepare some food. For the first time in over a month Rosamunde felt genuinely hungry.

A long, surprisingly pleasurable evening ensued. The couple didn't ask any more questions of a personal nature. They were very interested in England, however, and Pierre in particular was keen to enquire how the country had changed since he was there at school many years ago. During pudding – peaches and fresh cream – Rosamunde asked Pierre to explain the family connection. She was embarrassed to admit she knew little about the maternal side of her family. After Marguerite died, her father had found it painful to speak about her, and Granny Dupont had always been so unapproachable.

'My mother was called Delphine Dupont and she married Fabien Lacroix – my father,' he began. 'I'm afraid both my parents are now dead. But my mother had a brother called Laurent Dupont – your grandfather. He was in the French Air Force but was injured in a farming incident and had a false leg. He and his elderly parents moved to England when they saw the danger France was in – he was worried about caring for them if France became occupied. While he was there, in England, he discovered the Air Transport Auxiliary were desperate for pilots, tin leg or not. This was where he met your grandmother, Penelope, who was also in the ATA. Laurent was a wonderful uncle and he and your grandmother visited us all in France often after the war, even though they made their home in England. It was very tough for them, of course,' he added.

'Why?' asked Rosamunde.

'Well, your grandmother was from aristocracy. Her family owned a place called Hartley Hall in Dorset. When she met Laurent they fell madly in love, but her parents didn't approve. Then there was a scandal. Before they married, Penelope discovered she was pregnant. Of course she and Laurent married very quickly – a shotgun wedding, I think you call it. But her parents disinherited Penelope and all their wealth was left to her brother Charles, a very unpleasant man who refused to help his sister.'

Rosamunde took a sip of coffee. She was staggered – fancy her grandmother getting pregnant out of wedlock. But now she thought about it, perhaps that explained how kind she'd been to Rosamunde, in a most out-of-character fashion, when she'd found herself pregnant as a teenager.

'Laurent was not a man of wealth – we are not an especially rich family – and of course Penelope was used to a different way of living. But she was sufficiently in love with Laurent not to resent the loss of wealth and they were very happy together. I remember they would stay with us and all you could hear was their laughter, wherever you were in the house.'

Rosamunde frowned. This didn't sound like her grandmother at all. She'd barely seen her laugh over the years. When she'd hugged her grandmother goodbye Rosamunde remembered feeling sad that her life had been so devoid of joy. Pierre noticed Rosamunde's confusion.

'In later years she has not been so happy. But believe me, back then she was full of laughter and joy.' He smiled at the memories. 'She was so good with children. I was a small boy and she was always embracing me and trying to teach me English. It was Penelope who suggested I attend school in England, and even though it was very expensive my parents scrimped and saved to do so – to give me an excellent education for which I've always been most grateful. Without it I would not have my decent job as a wine merchant or this house and most certainly not a swimming pool!' he laughed.

'What happened, then, to my grandmother to change her so much?' asked Rosamunde as she stifled a yawn. It was dark now and the cicadas were chirruping their nighttime chorus. It had been a long day.

'There's so much more to tell,' Pierre told her. 'I think perhaps you should get some rest. We have all the time in the world. I'll continue with the story tomorrow evening. I have to work tomorrow but Cecile will look after you. You must make yourself at home, enjoy the pool.'

Rosamunde stood up. 'Thank you,' she said and it was a *thank you* that needed to cover so much.

'It is our pleasure,' he told her earnestly. 'You must stay here as long as you want. Sleep well.'

As she lay in the foreign bed in the guest room, under old-fashioned sheets, Rosamunde felt exhausted but her mind was awhirl with unanswered questions. As she began eventually to nod off, she wondered if her grandmother had sent Rosamunde to her nephew not just to heal her broken heart but perhaps finally to learn about her mysterious family history. Or perhaps her grandmother, wise though austere, believed the former could somehow partly be achieved by the latter.

37.
CHRISTMAS EVE 2014

At five o'clock in the morning on Christmas Eve Rosamunde woke up with a dreadful sore throat and a high fever. She took some paracetamol and went back to sleep, but when she woke again a few hours later she felt little better although her fever was down. She groaned. Why did colds always strike at Christmas? But she refused to be defeated. In her mind Christmas Eve had always been the best bit of Christmas and there was a lot going on today. So she dosed herself up, took a steaming bath and dressed warmly. After applying a bit of make-up and drinking a hot toddy for breakfast, she began to feel more human.

Bernie was the next to appear in the kitchen and he sounded even croakier than Rosamunde.

'Oh no! Dad, you could do without this! Sit down. I'll make you a hot toddy too.'

'Thanks, Rosie. Not too strong. Lots to do today. Bloody throat always seems to go at Christmas.'

'I know; it's the damnedest time of year for it.'

They were sitting at the table nursing their drinks and croaking at one another when Mrs Garfield bustled in, taking off her coat whilst trilling *Silent Night*.

'Best day of Christmas!' she announced and then took one look at Bernie and Rosamunde and sent them back to bed. 'No need for you to be up yet, feeling so poorly. Back to bed, both of you, and I'll wake you in time for some hearty soup at lunch. Now, you're not to worry about all the arrangements. Rachel and I will get everything organised and the play doesn't start until four o'clock.'

As ordered, Bernie and Rosamunde retreated to their rooms. As Rosamunde propped herself up in bed and dozed, she enjoyed the sounds of daily life going on downstairs. It reminded her of being off school as a young child and listening to her mother set about homely chores such as vacuuming and washing, while she was tucked snugly in bed with a hot drink and some books. Now she could hear Simon shouting at the children to get their coats on and then the slam of the back door as he doubtless took them off on a walk down to the beach. Then, like old times, the hum of the Hoover began.

Rosamunde settled down to her book. But then, as the Hoover noise subsided, her ears pricked up again. There was a whis-tling noise and a thud as the post was delivered. Lots more cards by the sounds of it. She could hear Rachel and Mrs Garfield scream-ing with laughter over something or other. After that the noises drifted to the back of her subconscious and Rosamunde fell asleep. By the time she was awakened by Mrs Garfield at one o'clock she felt much better.

Her father, too, had more colour to his cheeks and they joined everyone around the table in the kitchen for thick vegetable soup with hunks of granary loaf. There wasn't enough room for the children and so they'd already eaten and had been permitted to play in the garden while the adults ate their lunch.

'More snow in the air by the looks of it,' remarked Simon as he wolfed down Mrs Garfield's delicious soup.

'Always a tricky one – so lovely for us but dreadful for anyone having to travel,' Rosamunde replied.

'You think far too much about other people,' laughed Rachel. 'It's about time we enjoyed a white Christmas! Our first family Christmas in fifteen years and I think snow would be the icing on the cake,' she declared.

Rosamunde smiled, then, moving on to practicalities, she asked, 'Now tell me, what still needs to be done this afternoon?'

'The sitting room's all ready, thanks to your sister – she's done a marvellous job decorating it – and once we've had lunch we can get the kitchen all spruce,' Mrs Garfield explained. 'Then we'll need to get down to the church hall for about three to start getting everything ready for the play. I'm leaving the back door open for the caterers to get started while we're out. Benedict has already set up the lighting and the stage is set so it's more a question of helping to get everyone ready. Simon, Benedict and Ed are in charge of bringing in the animals with Benedict's father's help. So kind of him to lend them to us.'

Everyone agreed it was and soon they were all up and about, clearing the kitchen. Rosamunde took a moment to inspect the sitting room and gasped with delight when she saw how Rachel had transformed it into a magical, festive grotto. White fairy lights were festooned in every conceivable nook and dozens of candles were scattered around, ready to be lit before the party began. The tree stood handsomely in the corner of the room, giving off a beautiful scent of pine, and the presents were scattered enticingly at the bottom of the tree. A table had been dragged in from the hallway and had gleaming, polished glasses arranged on it. The scene was set.

But for now the family gathered coats, hats and scarves and walked the short distance to the church hall, which was mayhem with children cavorting around playing tag and actors practising their lines. Rosamunde, Rachel and Kizzie were in charge of helping the children to get ready and soon the angels were suitably attired and the side room could be made available for the adult shepherds, kings and innkeeper to change. One of the kings couldn't find his frankincense but Benedict managed to locate it in the crib. Then the Baby Jesus arrived; thankfully, he was asleep.

'Long may that continue,' whispered Rachel, though not particularly quietly so that the baby's mother gave her a sharp look.

By half past three parishioners started to arrive. Benedict and Simon had just brought in a couple of reasonably biddable sheep and a cow and led them onto the stage (the donkey was staying outside for now) when Bernie emerged from the hall office looking flustered.

'Oh dear,' he complained. 'I've just had a call from Florence,' he told his daughters. 'She and Anna have had the most dreadful row and they've pulled out of the nativity play at the last minute. What on earth can we do at this late stage?'

'We'll just have to find a couple to replace them,' said Rosamunde as she craned her neck to see if there were any suitable people in the hall. The only couples who'd arrived so far looked far too old to pass for a young Mary and Joseph.

'Rachel?' she suggested. 'How about you and Simon?'

'I would, darling, but Simon wouldn't dream of it. You know he has that slight stutter? Well, it comes out dreadfully when he's nervous. He'd never forgive me if I made him do it. I do have an idea, though. Give me a minute.'

Rachel was off, down to the back of the hall in a whirl of red coat and cashmere hat and scarf. Two minutes later she was back, with Benedict in tow.

'Looks like we're a couple.' Benedict grinned at Rosamunde and winked cheekily.

'Oh no, no, no,' Rosamunde replied, but she was bundled off into the side room and promptly given a script to learn in twenty minutes flat. As she and Benedict rehearsed their lines, Kizzie and Rachel busily attired them in their outfits before disappearing to take their seats.

'Everyone ready?' asked Bernie as he poked his head around the door ten minutes later. 'It's a full house!' He glowed proudly.

'Great,' groaned Rosamunde. She'd never enjoyed being the centre of attention and here she was about to play Mary in front of a full house. She was still feeling quite put out when she peeked round the side of the stage and saw Kizzie, Gerard and the girls at the back of the hall looking brave and cheerful. It was the boot up the backside Rosamunde needed, and she decided to be gracious about her plight.

'You look beautiful as Mary,' Benedict whispered as he stroked her hand tenderly, and Rosamunde felt all the speedily learnt lines vanishing from her mind. Perhaps she wasn't quite over him after all. Rosamunde's heart began to pound with nerves mingled with her feelings for Benedict.

The couple then made their way down to the side door of the hall, where the donkey was waiting patiently for them in the darkening afternoon. Simon and Ed helped Rosamunde on and Benedict slowly led them into the hall. As the door slammed behind them the whole audience turned around to see Rosamunde, Benedict and the donkey gradually make their way up to the stage to the tune of *Little Donkey*. Although she still felt a bit of a fool Rosamunde had to admit to herself that there was a certain magic to the scene.

The play proceeded to go smoothly, with only the odd line forgotten by Mary and Joseph. One of the angels burst into tears when she saw her parents in the audience and Baby Jesus was a little restless, but all in all it was deemed a huge success. Or at least it was until the very end when one of the sheep started to make strange noises before collapsing noisily. Ed immediately dashed to the stage where he found the sheep had already died.

'What's wrong with the poor sheepy?' asked the tearful angel.

'Oh nothing, nothing, she's just having a little sleep,' Ed told her and the audience as they became restless in their seats. Bernie intervened, standing in front of the sheep, and told the crowd he thought the nativity play had been the best to date and that he was sure everyone would agree Benedict and Rosamunde had fulfilled the roles of Joseph and Mary beautifully at the last minute, to which there was enormous applause.

After the audience had bundled out of the hall and most of the actors had sloped off, Bernie returned to the sheep and Ed.

'Dead?' he asked.

'Afraid so,' replied Ed. 'And I think I might know the cause.' He lifted up some branches of yew tree that the flower arrangers had decorated the stage with to make it festive. 'Yew is poisonous to sheep, I'm afraid. I think this one may have got a little greedy. The ewe killed by the yew,' he smiled wryly.

Explanations had to follow, with Benedict's father being very patient and understanding. Meanwhile Rachel, Rosamunde and Benedict, after offering their condolences about the sheep, dashed back to the house to get changed and deal with last-minute preparations for the party, which was due to start in half an hour. Rosamunde spotted most of the party guests filtering into the pub and she guessed they would arrive already merry. It should be an interesting evening.

After checking that everything was in order with the caterers and asking Benedict to start lighting the candles, Rosamunde dashed upstairs where Rachel applied her make-up for her and expertly styled her hair. Then, as Rachel hurried off to get herself ready, Rosamunde pulled on black tights, high heels and her never-been-worn midnight blue strapless dress. It fitted like a dream. She wondered if there was any chance of beguiling Benedict tonight and, as she checked herself again in the mirror, Rosamunde decided it was now or never. If Benedict didn't fall for her tonight – with her hair and make-up beautifully crafted by Rachel and adorned in the most beautiful dress she'd ever worn – then it would never happen. As she started to descend the stairs she found herself needing to grab on to the banister. Her knees were trembling with anticipation.

38.
AUGUST 1999
FRANCE

The next day dawned and upon opening the shutters in her room Rosamunde discovered a flawless blue sky. She listened at the open window. The only sound was the chitter-chatter of bird song. She looked at her watch and was astonished to discover it was eleven o'clock.

'I'm sorry I slept so late,' she apologised to Cecile, who was scrubbing the kitchen floor. Cecile clearly didn't understand but she ushered Rosamunde through to the terrace where the table was laid for one, with a jug of orange juice and a basket of fresh bread. Rosamunde was touched. She sat down to tuck in and soon Cecile hurried out again with coffee.

'Relax! Enjoy!' she said before returning to her household tasks. Rosamunde felt guilty at being so idle when her hostess clearly took her job as housewife extremely seriously, so after breakfast she cleared the table and washed her plate and glass, then managed to locate Cecile dusting in the enormous salon. Rosamunde could imagine that the size of the villa must make the keeping of it a full-time job.

'Can I help at all?' asked Rosamunde, putting on a charade of vacuuming in an attempt to get her point across. Cecile looked astonished.

'No, no, no. Guest. You here as guest. You relax. Enjoy!' she said, smiling, before turning her back on Rosamunde to continue with her dusting. Rosamunde stayed where she was, unsure how to explain that she really would like to help, but a moment later Cecile was shooing her out of the room. Clearly she thought Rosamunde would be more of a hindrance than a help, so Rosamunde returned to her room, changed into a bikini, found her book and made her way down to the swimming pool.

By the end of the day Rosamunde had turned a shade darker, despite sitting mainly under a parasol, and her body and mind had well and truly wound down. She'd been keen not to allow herself too much time to think, so she'd almost finished the riveting novel she'd brought with her. She would have to locate a bookstore selling English books, as well as a place that sold sunglasses. Perhaps a trip to the nearest town in the next day or two was in order.

As Rosamunde showered in the early evening, the cool water heavenly on her sun-kissed skin, she marvelled at what a difference the change in location had made. She was still feeling bruised and hurt, but her desperation had been replaced with the beginnings of a sense of peace. Perhaps a place such as this made it impossible to feel too full of angst. She felt so grateful in that moment to her grandmother – that sharp, buttoned-up woman who she was now discovering had once been someone so different.

After supper she was desperate to find out more. Pierre handed her a coffee as Cecile cleared the plates and disappeared off to the kitchen.

'You would like to hear more about your grandmother, I think?' he asked.

'Please,' said Rosamunde. 'It's all so astonishing. You'll think it strange I don't know this history but I'm afraid my father doesn't like to talk about the past – he was so devastated by my mother's death. And Granny Dupont is nothing like the person you describe. She's always been very austere, so unapproachable.'

'It is a shame how life can change us,' Pierre remarked. 'I'm so glad I can fill in the gaps for you, anyway. It is important, is it not, to know our history?' Rosamunde agreed and sat back in her chair to listen.

'I explained to you how happy your grandmother was, married to Laurent. They married in October 1945 and your mother was born that December. After the war they remained in England. Laurent found a job as a farmhand, and they lived in the country in a tiny little cottage. Any money they saved they used to visit us in France. Your mother was a beautiful baby, thriving in the country air. To earn a few pennies Penelope helped local children with their schoolwork and when Marguerite started school Penelope began work as a teacher at the same place. They were a happy family. Simple, but happy. And then one day, there was a terrible accident. You must know that Laurent was run over by a tractor?' Rosamunde nodded. This much her father had told her and it had always struck her as the most abysmal way to die.

'They say lightning never strikes twice but for Laurent it did – first the accident with his leg; then the fatal incident with the tractor. After that, it was very hard for Penelope. She and your mother had to move out of their cottage – it came with Laurent's job. She appealed to her parents for help, but they were stubborn and refused to let their daughter back into their life or even to meet little Marguerite. Penelope had a job at the school now and so she had a little money, but without Laurent's wage it was very tough. She and Marguerite moved in with another teacher from the school for a while, but it was barely ideal as the house was already cramped with her colleague's family.

'Penelope continued to write to my parents with her news and, though she tried to sound cheerful, it was clear to them she was heartbroken and very poor. So my parents saved up and sent across the money for Penelope and Marguerite to travel to France. I remember they arrived with so few possessions in September 1951. The first thing I noticed was that Penelope no longer laughed. Even when my father cracked jokes – and they were good jokes – she never laughed.

'But she was a strong lady and she made a life for herself over here. Marguerite attended school and was soon bilingual, and Penelope found work teaching English. They lived with us for some time until Penelope found a small place to rent and they moved out, but they were always nearby. Although Penelope was not the same person she had been, she always had time for me, and Marguerite was as cute as a button.'

Pierre paused to take a sip of espresso. Rosamunde was engrossed in the story. It was so precious to hear about her mother's life, to be able to build a picture of the young girl who became such a wonderful mother for seven years of Rosamunde's life. It was like watching an enormous jigsaw puzzle start to take shape – pictures that had once been so hazy suddenly becoming clear.

'So they made their home here and at one point Penelope did have the opportunity to move on from her grief. There was a man in the village – Yves – a lovely man. He pursued your grandmother for some time, but she had closed her heart. Eventually he gave up and married a local girl. At around this time Penelope decided she was missing England too much and they moved back to the West Country. I don't know if she regretted her decision about Yves. Penelope took a job in a private school teaching French and working as a housemistress and Marguerite had a free place at the school. And so Penelope devoted the rest of her life to teaching and, of course, later on to helping raise you and your sister. Unfortunately I believe she has never been truly happy since those days with Laurent, especially after Marguerite died as well. How can a person be fully happy without love?'

At this Rosamunde felt a sharp stab of pain. Did the death of love have to mean a lonely, embittered life? The thought was terrifying. She didn't want to end up like her grandmother. But then she thought of Bernie – he'd never found anyone to replace Marguerite but it hadn't changed him. He was so soft and full of love and gentleness. Rosamunde sighed and focused again on Pierre.

'So we didn't see them again for some time. The next time I saw my cousin – Marguerite – she was sixteen!' Pierre paused. 'But look, your mother is a whole other story. It's late. Let's get to bed. I'll tell you all about darling Marguerite tomorrow.'

39.
CHRISTMAS EVE 2014

The sound of a champagne cork popping always sets the scene for the start of a party and, upon hearing that delicious pop, Rosamunde entered the sitting room where she found the popper himself – Benedict – standing over the table of gleaming glasses. He looked at her and paused in his pouring.

'Bloody hell, Rosamunde!' he exclaimed. 'I hardly recognised you,' he teased. Rosamunde pulled a face and helped herself to a glass of fizz, all the better to embolden her.

Next to join them was Rachel who was already adorned in her burlesque outfit and looked very saucy indeed, with her milky white cleavage on display and the rest of her body encased in a tight emerald green outfit that was little more than a swimming costume with tassels.

'Doesn't she look amazing?' asked Simon, always in awe of his beautiful wife. She planted a juicy kiss on his lips in gratitude.

Next to arrive in the sitting room were Bernie and Mrs Garfield, looking and smelling delicious, and there was that nervous moment just before a party begins when the hosts wonder if it will be a success or not. And then the doorbell rang and any worries were quickly washed away in the tide of greetings that followed, as each new guest entered speckled with the snowflakes that had just started to fall.

The crowded cottage was soon bursting with life and laughter, as the revellers became pinker and pinker with champagne. Soon the food was brought round by Kizzie's older daughters and the guests were able to soak up some of the alcohol with the festive fare. Christmas carols played in the background although they were drowned out for the most part by the chatter and laughter that filled the house.

At about ten o'clock there was the clinking of knife on glass as Simon asked everyone to clear a space in the sitting room for his wife's performance. A moment later the carols had been exchanged for the introductory bars of *Big Spender* and Rachel appeared with a chair from the kitchen, behind which she stood with a saucy pout and a jiggling hip. The dance that ensued was astonishingly well executed and very sensuous, raising the temperature in the sitting room even higher than it was already. At the end of the routine, as Rachel sashayed onto the chair, spread her legs and tipped her head over so her red curls fell to the floor, the applause was deafening.

'Encore, encore!' the guests chanted and Rachel began a second dance to *New York, New York*. Halfway through she decided to drag Rosamunde and Mrs Garfield up to join in, much to Rosamunde's horror. But she'd had enough to drink to make her game and joined in as best she could, laughing at the wolf-whistles, while Mrs Garfield surprised everyone with her agility.

Afterwards Rachel was immediately on to Mrs G, persuading her she should take up classes as a way of keeping fit.

'I don't think they have classes around here for burlesque,' chuckled Mrs G. 'Marjorie Hawson has been doing her legs, bums and tums for twenty years and she's not a great one for change,' she added.

Soon most of the partygoers, including Kizzie and Gerard, started to dance. Rosamunde spotted Ed whirling Alison Thacker around the sitting room to Don McLean's *American Pie* and was glad to see her enjoying herself at what must have felt like the most painful of Christmases – her first without Richard.

Rosamunde decided to sneak upstairs to check her make-up and, on her way, bumped into Bernie in the hallway. He'd just downed a black coffee to counteract the champagne and was about to head over to the church for Midnight Mass.

'Okay, Dad?' she asked, hugging him to her.

'Excellent, excellent. Just been making sure I can say "vicissitudes" for the service, and I can. My sobriety test,' he chuckled as he disengaged himself from Rosamunde to pop his dog collar on.

'I don't think you'll have many takers from the party,' remarked Rosamunde, as she made her way up the stairs. 'It's still in full swing!' she laughed.

'Make sure there's some drink left for when I get back!' called Bernie, and he wove his way through the crowded cottage to head across to the church.

Once upstairs, Rosamunde was taken by surprise when she turned to shut her bedroom door and found Benedict had followed her up.

'Am I interrupting?' he asked.

'No, of course not. Come in,' she said.

'I just wanted to catch you on your own for a moment to give you this,' Benedict explained, producing with a flourish a gift inexpertly wrapped in festive paper. 'I know I'm seeing you tomorrow but I suspect it'll be chaos and I wanted to see you open it.' He grinned sheepishly.

'You're not going to put me to shame, are you?' she asked. 'I'm afraid I've only got you the ski socks you asked for!'

'Just open it!' he ordered. So Rosamunde perched on the edge of the bed and unpeeled the wrapping to discover the most exquisite clay koala painted in the most glorious orange and red hues, the details outlined in delicate gold. It was the most beautiful object Rosamunde had ever been given. She was speechless, but her tear-filled eyes said it all. Benedict looked at her enquiringly then took the koala and placed it carefully on the bedside table before sitting on the bed and taking Rosamunde's face in his hands.

The kiss felt bizarrely familiar, as if they had been kissing all their lives, but it was no less wonderful for it. They fitted, Rosamunde thought, and she wondered what on earth had taken them so long.

The party immediately forgotten, they didn't emerge from Rosamunde's bedroom until the following morning. When Rosamunde awoke to find Benedict beside her she found herself astonished at just how right it felt. She lay there watching his long fluttering eyelashes until there was a loud crash and Lily and Art burst into the bedroom, waking Benedict and causing Rosamunde to pull the duvet up to cover her modesty.

'There's a man in your bed!' remarked Lily. 'It's not Father Christmas, is it?' she asked, peering to get a better view. Rosamunde laughed.

'No, s'my friend Benlict,' Art told his sister, knowledgeably.

'So sorry.' The next to burst in was Rachel. 'They were dying to say Happy Christmas,' grinned Rachel. Then she spotted Benedict. 'Oh, yikes! Gosh! Sorry. No idea. Out, out, children. Now, quick, quick!' and the three reversed out of the bedroom.

'I guess there's no chance of this being a secret union, then,' remarked Benedict with a raised eyebrow, before turning to kiss Rosamunde. She kissed him back and, as a result, the couple arrived late, dishevelled and snow-flecked at the morning service.

'You devil! I thought he was gay! Top marks for the conversion,' whispered Rachel as the pair joined the others in the Vicarage pew, everyone budging up to accommodate them.

'Ssshh!' replied Rosamunde, though she could hardly contain her happiness. She sang merrily along with all the carols and dug Benedict in the ribs during his dreadful descant in *O Come All Ye Faithful.* Rachel also revealed her New Year's resolution to Rosamunde during this final hymn.

'I've decided to be faithful from now on,' she told her sister. 'I've finished things with my Spanish lover. I think it's time to focus on Simon.'

Rosamunde was amazed but pleased and Simon winked at her. She wondered how much of a blind eye he'd had to turn over the years. *What is it about this Christmas?* she wondered to herself. *Could there be any more surprises?*

As it turned out, there was another one in store.

40.
AUGUST 1999
FRANCE

After a day trip to the nearest town – beautiful but hideously busy and stiflingly hot – Rosamunde returned to the peace and tranquillity of the villa. As had become their custom so quickly and easily, Rosamunde joined her hosts for an aperitif followed by a delicious dinner. And after dinner – as had also become their habit – Pierre continued with his storytelling.

'Your mother,' he said, twinkling at Rosamunde. 'Now, she was the most glorious person ever to live on this planet. Why is it always the case that the most wonderful creatures die early and the most horrible of people seem to survive forever?' he asked, and Rosamunde thought how true that was.

'She wasn't perfect, though, of course,' he added. 'But you name one human being who is,' he said, and Rosamunde found her interest piqued. Of course, in her mind her mother was the most perfect person ever to have existed. She was interested to have an insight into the fuller picture.

'I think I told you I didn't see Marguerite until she was sixteen. She came to visit us then, and my goodness, was she beautiful!

I must admit I fell a little bit in love with her myself. And she was so full of beauty within as well. Her eyes – dark eyes – they gleamed with her life and vitality. I tell you, she brought some much-needed glamour to our village and caused quite a stir. The boys of the village were tripping over themselves in their desperate pursuit of her, but Marguerite, while she was friendly, remained a little aloof. You see, as well as being vital and engaging, she had this serenity about her, too. I see this in you, Rosamunde, this gentle serenity. It is the most attractive of qualities.'

Rosamunde blushed, delighted with the compliment and the comparison to her mother.

'One of the most striking things about Marguerite was her beautiful wardrobe of clothes. She had little money, of course, but she had learnt to sew at school and by sixteen she was the most accomplished dressmaker, making all her own clothes. She looked a million dollars and it was a real passion for her. When she was staying with us, very often she would work on patterns late into the night and spend the days stitching whilst she gossiped with my mother.'

Rosamunde nodded. She remembered how her mother had always been beautifully turned out, her clothes the perfect expression of her character – elegant, beautiful and a little playful too.

'It was on this visit to France when she was sixteen that an old friend of my father came to visit. He lived in Paris and when he discovered Marguerite's skill he suggested she should try to find an apprenticeship at a design house in France. I think your mother had given little thought to her future at that point, although she had just left school. Suddenly she was seized with the desire to pursue such a career and within a year she'd won herself an apprenticeship at Chanel! Her ambition was astonishing in those days – this was 1962 – and she was all alone in Paris. Penelope was in Exeter and Marguerite knew no one at all to start with. But she could speak the language and she adored the job, working incredibly long hours but making many friends as well. Now and then she would take a short break and visit us here, regaling us with all the stories of the glamour and the fashion shows.'

Rosamunde smiled. She knew this part of the story but it was wonderful to hear it again after so many years. When Rosamunde was small she had insisted her mother tell her all about her days of working in Paris – she never tired of the story, thinking it amazing her mother could once have been somebody other than her mother.

'A couple of years later, with her apprenticeship under her belt, Marguerite returned to England for a short trip to see her mother. Her relationship with Penelope was not brilliant. Penelope was fearful her daughter would make the same mistakes she had made – for by now she was rather bitter about the fact she'd disobeyed her parents to take off with Laurent. She'd begun to forget how in love she had been with him and found herself wishing she hadn't rebelled. This made her over-protective of Marguerite, although, of course, she had little control over her by this point and Marguerite was very headstrong.

'Anyway, she still loved her mother – of course – and so she had returned for a short visit. It was during this trip that she met Bernie. They were both nineteen and he had just started studying theology at Exeter University after a brief spell working in a bank. It was a pretty new university back then. They met in a pub one evening and a whirlwind romance followed. But, of course, the time came when Marguerite had to return to her job in Paris and Bernie had three years of study left. They agreed to keep in touch by letter, which they did, but it wasn't long before Marguerite was swept off her feet again. This time by a man called Etienne.'

Rosamunde was agog. This was a part of the tale she was not familiar with.

'Your mother was treated badly by this man. He was what I think the English call a "cad". But she was smitten with him – she adored him. Then, like history repeating itself, she found herself pregnant.' Rosamunde took a sharp intake of breath.

'She was pregnant?' she asked, almost unable to believe her ears. Suddenly she found herself quite dizzy with concern. She tried very quickly to do the maths. It must by now have been the mid-1960s. Did this mean Rachel was only a half sister? She took a gulp of wine and waited – with bated breath – for the next instalment of the story.

41.
CHRISTMAS DAY 2014

After church, Benedict returned to Farm Cottage to change his clothes. Ed was still in bed so Benedict shouted at him to meet in the pub in half an hour and asked him to bring Humphrey, who was enjoying a doze and clearly didn't want to be disturbed yet.

Rosamunde was already in The Dragon's Head with all the family when Benedict returned and, when he saw that his parents and Kizzie, Gerard and the girls were there as well, he decided it was time to reveal all. He ordered a pint of bitter and bravely turned to face his loved ones. He cleared his throat.

'Could I just say a few words, please?' he asked, adopting the booming voice Rosamunde remembered from that day of rehearsals in the church hall. She looked up, astonished. What on earth was he doing? His family, friends and half the pub silenced themselves to hear what Benedict had to say.

'As you know, for the last three years I've been gay. Or at least, I haven't actually been gay. I've been pretending to be gay.' A few gasps were audible around the pub, followed by the scrape of a chair. The next thing Rosamunde saw was a flash of blonde hair before Benedict received a stinging slap across the face.

'You bastard!' yelled Clara, before running out of the pub in tears. She was followed by a bewildered-looking husband, carrying a screeching Hugo.

'Shit, I didn't realise Clara was in the pub,' Benedict continued, putting a hand to his blazing red cheek. 'Well, I may as well continue now she's gone. Erm, so, where was I? I'm sorry I had to do it, but I had my reasons – which I'll explain another time. The point is that I'm not gay. And not only that, I'm in love with a woman.'

At this there were more gasps, as everyone looked around trying to determine who the mystery woman might be. Rachel smiled smugly to herself, being the only person aware of just who it was at the centre of this drama. Rachel always loved a good drama.

'Bloody hell, Benedict,' piped up Kizzie. 'Who's the woman?'

'Erm, well, actually it's Rosamunde,' he beamed, crossing the pub to take hold of her hand. 'It's official!' he announced. 'We're a couple!'

A round of applause followed, with Mrs Garfield contributing some loud wolf-whistles. Kizzie looked at her best friend, agog. She marched over.

'And when were you going to tell me?' she asked, sternly. Rosamunde felt like one of her pupils.

'I'm sorry,' she said. 'But it only happened last night!' At this, Kizzie's face softened and she clasped Rosamunde into a hug.

'I'm so pleased,' her friend told her. 'Truly, some good news like this is just what we all need.'

A moment later Ed entered the pub. He bought himself a beer and a packet of crisps for Humphrey before joining the rest of the group.

'Did I miss anything?' he asked and everyone began to laugh.

'Not much!' yelped Rachel, dabbing at her eyes.

There followed a hearty Christmas lunch at the Vicarage, which was eaten in the sitting room at the kitchen table (dragged through from the kitchen), to which had been added a garden table to make enough room for everyone. After this the group made their way down to Outer Cove to watch the Christmas Day swimmers. Every year a small posse of stalwarts went for a dip on Christmas Day afternoon and today Simon, Ed and Benedict decided to join in, much to the amusement of the rest of the group. They didn't last very long and emerged blue and shivering. Rosamunde wrapped Benedict in a large towel and hugged him to her.

'You didn't even swim!' she admonished him.

'It was too cold,' he told her, his teeth chattering. 'And to be honest, I'm not the greatest swimmer at the best of times.'

'Well, if you do this next year, at least wear a wetsuit,' she laughed as they all hotfooted it back through the snow to the Vicarage to warm up with tea and crumpets.

It was at this point that Bernie asked to see Rachel and Rosamunde in his study and they instantly feared the worst. Immediately Rosamunde decided he must be ill. This was going to be a horrible surprise – she felt it in her bones.

'Sit down, girls,' Bernie ordered, looking serious. 'I have something to tell you and I hope you won't find this too difficult.' Rosamunde's heart sank further into her boots.

'The thing is . . .' he explained, looking anxious, 'I've asked Mrs Garfield to marry me and she's said yes.' Rosamunde thought she might burst with delighted shock.

'I know this is going to be hard for you both but she won't in any way replace your mother. It's just that we've become very fond of each other over the years and we're such good companions . . .' He stopped.

'Dad, don't be ridiculous!' Rosamunde admonished. 'We're in our forties now – we're not kids – and of course we don't mind. It's the best news we could have hoped for,' she said, hugging her father.

'Fabulous news!' grinned Rachel. 'Where the hell is Mrs G?' she asked. 'We need to talk dresses!'

'She's in the kitchen, I should think. Oh, I'm so pleased you don't mind! I've been so worried about telling you both.'

'You're so daft!' said Rosamunde. 'But there is one thing, Dad,' she added. Bernie looked up, concerned.

'Yes?'

'Well, if she's going to be our stepmother we can't keep calling her Mrs Garfield. What on earth's her real name?'

'Ah, yes,' Bernie smiled. 'It's a habit I must get out of myself! She's called Elizabeth Anne,' he told his daughters. 'But she's asked us to call her Betty.'

Yes, thought Rosamunde. *Betty Pemberton.* That seemed to her the perfect name for dear Mrs G.

❦

The evening that followed entailed a raucous game of charades followed by bedtime for the children and *Love Actually* for the adults, who'd all seen it before, apart from Rosamunde. She was the only person who managed to stay awake until the end, at which point she dragged Benedict up to bed. As they lay in each other's arms she suddenly remembered that Benedict was leaving the next day for his month in France.

'What time do you leave tomorrow?' she asked.

'Lunchtime,' Benedict replied, grinning ruefully at her. 'I wish I wasn't going now. Can you be tempted to come with me?'

'I wish I could but I've my new job at the wildlife park to start next week,' she told him, rueful herself that, having finally got together, they now had to endure a month apart.

'Well, you'd better not go off me in the next month,' Benedict told her, planting a kiss on her mouth. 'Now that I've come round to the idea of not being a bachelor for the rest of my life, I don't think I can bear to lose you,' he added more seriously. 'I can't tell you how relieved I was that you weren't interested in Ed after all. When you asked me to fix you up on a date with him I was gutted.'

'Well, you should have told me you had feelings for me sooner! I had no idea you felt the same way as me!' Rosamunde exclaimed. Benedict looked sheepish.

'I was going to,' he admitted. 'The day I explained to you why I'd been pretending to be gay. But then everyone came back in from the snow and the moment was lost. I'd been trying to pluck up the courage ever since and when I saw you again last night I knew I couldn't waste any more time.'

Rosamunde squeezed him to her. It was a funny thing. They'd both reached a stage in their lives where they'd been quite content to remain single and suddenly they had found each other. It was quite a turnaround, but now it had happened it seemed to Rosamunde it had somehow always been destined.

∾

The next morning was full of goodbyes. Ed was off to London to see his children but he confided in Rosamunde that he was quite taken with Alison Thacker and would be looking for excuses to return soon.

Then it was time for Benedict to leave. The goodbyes were hard, but it was with a sense of peace that Rosamunde watched him and Humphrey drive off. It might only have been December but Rosamunde felt like a spring flower, slowly unfurling after a long winter.

'Keep safe!' she called out into the distance and the Land Rover hooted in reply.

42.
AUGUST 1999
FRANCE

'You needn't panic,' Pierre assured Rosamunde. 'I'm afraid your mother lost her first baby, the same as you.'

Rosamunde took a deep breath. Thank heavens. She had been dreading the thought of having to tell Rachel that Bernie wasn't actually her father, but then she thought of her sister's red hair – just like her own and an obvious characteristic inherited from Bernie – and she realised she'd never had cause to worry.

'By this time Etienne had left Marguerite high and dry and your mother was utterly heartbroken. She decided to return to Exeter, leaving her glittering career behind, but she soon swapped her life of glamour for the love of a good man. You mustn't think she just settled for Bernie, though. She really did love him. I think the affair with Etienne cemented those feelings in the end. And, of course, you know the rest. Your parents married, Bernie started his first job as a vicar in Potter's Cove and soon Rachel was on the way. When you were a baby you all came to stay with us in France and we had the most wonderful time. I don't think I'd ever seen a couple so right for each other as your parents. It doesn't surprise me your father has never found anyone else. How could anyone compare to Marguerite?'

It was true and yet Rosamunde was brought back to thinking about this pattern of love only striking once in her family. There was her grandmother and then there was Bernie. Both of them had loved once and never again. The thought that she would follow this pattern terrified her.

Rosamunde left France the following week, after a tearful farewell with her kindly hosts, with a ticket to India, her suitcase and a newfound knowledge of her family history, which had left her certain of one thing. She might never fall in love again but she was determined that she would not follow in her grandmother's footsteps and be forever unhappy and embittered. Instead she would do her best to be like her father – she would seek out peace and joy and love, even if she remained single for the rest of her days.

Had this been her grandmother's intention when she sent Rosamunde to France? Was this the lesson she'd hoped Rosamunde would learn? Rosamunde would never find out, for Granny Dupont died a week later of a heart attack. Rosamunde returned to Exeter briefly for the funeral, but hardly saw her family after that for fifteen years, visiting very briefly for Rachel and Simon's wedding and later to see her niece and nephew shortly after Art was born. She missed them all dreadfully but there was something that prevented her from returning home. There was a journey Rosamunde needed to embark on and in the depth of her soul she knew she couldn't go back for good until there was some signal – some indication that the journey was over.

The years were full of adventures and lovers, but Rosamunde didn't settle anywhere until she reached Perth – a place that she wasn't sure she would ever leave, she loved it so much. There was also the draw of Troy Daniels, the toy boy she'd met there. It was never serious, though, and when the recurring dreams began Rosamunde knew the signal she'd expected had arrived.

It was time to go home.

43.
JANUARY 2015

Of course, the path of true love never did run smoothly and it would have been too much to hope, thought Rosamunde ruefully, that she might at last have found a relationship that would play out without any sort of drama at all.

Two weeks into their separation, after daily telephone calls, Rosamunde was surprised to get to the end of a working day without hearing from Benedict. She supposed he must have been on the slopes and without a mobile signal all day and thought nothing more of it until the next day arrived – a Saturday – and still she'd heard nothing. It was then she began, very quietly, to panic. She tried calling but there was no dialling tone on his mobile. They'd been speaking more than once a day and their conversations had been perfectly cheerful, with no arguments, so Rosamunde was left to surmise that one of three things had happened: Benedict had suddenly got cold feet about their relationship, or he'd been kidnapped, or he was in some other sort of trouble. She thought it unlikely really that he'd been kidnapped, which left just two options: he wanted nothing more to do with her, or he'd had an accident.

All of a sudden Rosamunde was reminded of those bleak days in the aftermath of the Zeebrugge disaster, when she'd been in limbo, waiting to find out whether Stephen was all right while certain he was not. This time Rosamunde was determined not to be so passive in the face of a crisis. She immediately booked a flight to Geneva, leaving that afternoon, and packed a bag. Her father was at Mrs G's (no, Betty's) house and so she left him a scrawled note, trying not to be too alarmist, and called a taxi. By five o'clock that afternoon she'd landed in Geneva.

There followed a most frustrating hour in which Rosamunde tried to hire a car and, finally having done so, descended into a hell-hole beneath the airport where she located the Renault and set about manoeuvring herself out of the car park while frustrated drivers beeped loudly at each other and two or three individuals crunched their cars as they tried to park in the too-tight spaces.

This was before Rosamunde had even started her journey in the dark, driving on the wrong side of the road, and unsure of her route. However, finally – and late at night – she arrived in Chamonix Mont-Blanc. It was only as she navigated her way into the town that she realised she had no idea where Benedict was staying. He'd never given her the address. Close to tears with frustration and fatigue, Rosamunde checked herself into a small chalet hotel and laid her weary head to rest for the night. Her emergency search would have to commence in the morning. And she still had no idea if she was searching for a man who wanted to be found.

The next day Rosamunde discovered the answer to that question. She decided she would have to start with the rather dreadful prospect of driving to the nearest hospital to rule out her most feared explanations for Benedict's sudden lack of contact. Her minimal French posed a few problems but soon after arriving at the hospital she was astonished to find the receptionist saying to her, 'Please follow me.' Immediately her ears began to pound with panic. Benedict was here?

She was led into a small room that had just enough room for a bed, a chair and a bedside locker. And there, lying prone on the bed, with a bandage wrapped around his skull and a leg in traction, was Benedict. His eyes were closed and he looked terrible.

'I'll get a doctor,' whispered the receptionist. Tentatively Rosamunde approached the bed and stroked Benedict's hand. He didn't move at all and his skin felt damp and cold. A feeling of dread crept over her entire body.

'You are Benedict's girlfriend, I believe?' came a voice from behind her. Rosamunde looked around and nodded.

'He had a terrible skiing accident the day before yesterday,' the doctor explained in fluent English. 'He's suffered a head injury, which we're keeping an eye on, but it's not as serious as we first thought. A badly broken leg, but he'll recover. He's on a lot of medication so he's sleeping a lot. I'm afraid he's groggy, making little sense. He keeps saying the name Humphrey so we thought maybe he had a male partner?' Rosamunde almost smiled at the irony.

'I'm afraid he had no phone with him,' continued the doctor. 'So we didn't know who to contact. Perhaps it was lost in the accident. Anyway, I'm pleased you made it.' A moment later the doctor was gone.

A little while later Rosamunde saw Benedict begin to stir.

'Benedict?' she said. 'It's me, Rosamunde.' Benedict opened his eyes and she saw two things in those dark pools: love and relief. He smiled and then grimaced.

'Humphrey,' he croaked. 'At the chalet. Hungry,' he managed and a tear slid down his cheek. Rosamunde understood immediately and her heart ached as she realised how anxious he must have been about Humphrey since the accident and how helpless he'd been to make anyone understand him.

'I'll go now,' she told him. 'Tell me the address,' she said, jotting his brief instructions down on a receipt from her bag. 'I'll feed

Humphrey and let him out. Then I'll be back.' She started to gather her things together. 'One thing, though,' Rosamunde added, smiling wryly. 'Is it the same leg you broke last time?' Benedict shook his head.

'Well, that's something, anyway. Now you stay here,' Rosamunde ordered and Benedict raised his eyebrows in pained amusement. And there, in that moment, Rosamunde knew. She knew, absolutely, that Benedict would be all right.

And she knew, without a doubt, that her heart had finally opened again – fully, completely and entirely. It seemed, after all, that love – real, proper, honest-to-goodness love – *could* strike more than once in a lifetime.

EPILOGUE
APRIL 2015

It was the day before Bernie's wedding and unseasonably warm. A day for the beach, even at this time of year. Rosamunde was lying on a towel rubbing her belly, her face tilted to the sun, while Benedict, now fully recovered and clad in a wetsuit, took his body board out to play around in the surf. As soon as he emerged from the sea she was going to tell him the news. She'd already shared it with Humphrey, who'd wagged his tail obligingly. He now lay beside her, his dubious breath a little too close to her nose.

Rosamunde turned from the sun to look out into the ocean beyond and was surprised to see a large black cloud looming on the horizon. She checked to see where Benedict was and grinned as she saw him waving at her, mucking about. Then, as the dark cloud moved closer, she realised he wasn't waving in jest. He was in trouble.

A moment later she was pounding down to the shore and ripping through the waves to reach him. As the blue sky became smothered entirely in black, Rosamunde reached Benedict. He was by now flailing around in a mad panic, swallowing huge gulps of water before submerging again. For the first time in her life

Rosamunde put to use the life-saving qualification she'd received when she was nine.

Minutes later, as they dragged themselves out of the water and, spluttering, made their way up the beach in the pouring rain, Rosamunde turned to Benedict and grabbed him to her in a fierce hug.

'They say these things happen in threes,' said Benedict, shaking the water out of his ears. 'A car crash, a skiing accident and now nearly drowning. I hope that's it!' he laughed in shock.

Then, suddenly, realisation dawned. Rosamunde held Benedict back from her and looked into his large, dark eyes. He returned her gaze quizzically.

'It was you I needed to save,' she told him in wonder, the puzzle of her recurring dreams finally solved. The dreams that had drawn her home again after so long away. Rosamunde shivered at their power. She pulled Benedict back into her arms.

'It was *you.*'

AUTHOR'S NOTE

All characters and storylines contained in this novel are fictional and any similarity with real life is purely coincidental.

ACKNOWLEDGEMENTS

This novel is in memory of my late father, the Reverend John Lambourne, who was an inspiration in so many ways and who thankfully had the opportunity to read it in draft, if not in published form. It is also written for my girls – Ruby and Iris.

My gratitude goes to Dad (Diddle), the late Granny Green, my husband Dan, my mum Lorna, and my siblings – Matt Lambourne, Kate Mannion and Vix Atkinson. I received a lot of encouragement and useful feedback from my family, as well as from a number of friends – Kirsty and Robin Pilcher, Elizabeth Kilgarriff, Natalie Willmott, Ruth Faye, Emma O'Prey, Kathryn Mills, Jessica Bouteloup, Sarah Lambourne, Helen Alkin and Bianca O'Connor.

Finally, my thanks also go to Jodi Warshaw at Lake Union Publishing for discovering my book and to Emilie Marneur, Sophie Missing, Jennifer McIntyre and the rest of the team at Amazon Publishing, who were a joy to work with.

ABOUT THE AUTHOR

Rebecca Boxall was born in East Sussex in 1977 and grew up in a bustling vicarage always filled with family, friends and parishioners. She now lives by the sea in Jersey with her husband and two children. She read English at the University of Warwick before training as a lawyer and also studied Creative Writing with The Writer's Bureau. *Christmas at the Vicarage* is her first novel.

For the latest author updates, you can follow Rebecca at:

www.rebeccaboxall.co.uk

www.facebook.com/christmasatthevicarage